TORN BETWEEN BAE AND THE THUG NEXT DOOR

TWYLA T.
J. DOMINIQUE

Torn Between Bae & The Thug Next Door

❀ Created with Vellum

MAILING LIST

To stay up to date on new releases, plus get information on contests, sneak peeks, and more,
Click The Link Below...

http://bit.ly/2BtGCXH

❧ 1 ❧

Mercedes guzzled down the shot of Patron she held and motioned to the bartender for another, unfazed by the slight burn it caused in her chest. It was her best friend's birthday and she planned on getting wasted and shaking her ass regardless of the consequences. The brief thought of the punishment she would receive from the night out sent a shudder rippling through her body, and she quickly threw back her second shot welcoming the way it erased her fear if only for a minute. She'd made sure to leave her tab open because she was going to put it to good use.

"Ayeee... this my shit bitch!" Her bestie Kiyah yelled in her ear as The City Girls song "Act Up" started blasting through the club's speakers. On cue, every female in the building rapped along. Kiyah grabbed Mercedes' hand and pulled her out onto the dance floor eagerly.

"Same group of bitches, ain't no adding to the picture! Drop a couple racks, watch this ass get bigger! Aye!" Both girls sang in unison as they twerked. Usually, Mercedes was extremely quiet and reserved per the demand of her fiancé Jermaine, or Maine as the streets called him. But a mixture of alcohol and her best friend brought out her true carefree and fun personality. She pulled down the bottom of her black strapless bodycon dress, and it rose right back up as she continued to shake her

ass against Kiyah. They danced to three songs until they were sweating and out of breath. Parched, the two made their way back over to the bar, shaking off the many men in the building that were trying to grab them and get their attention.

"Get them whatever they want Rita, everything on the house all night." Some guy said, sliding in next to Kiyah with a grin. She rolled her eyes and Mercedes hid her own smile, knowing that her girl wasn't about to give dude no play.

"No thank you, I can pay for my own drinks." Kiyah quipped and turned back to the bartender. "Two Long Islands and keep them on my tab please."

"Ohhhh, so you independent huh? I like that, but that's *my* employee so she's gone do what I tell her. Close the tab and charge the house." The guy smirked and Mercedes raised her brow. This nigga clearly wasn't taking no for an answer, and Mercedes could already tell that she was going to like him for her stubborn friend. Kiyah, on the other hand, frowned, ready to put his rude ass in his place.

"Look--"

"Major." He cut her off still with that same amused look on his face.

"What?" Kiyah's lip curled irritably.

"My name. It's Major." Mercedes looked back and forth between the two as she sipped her drink, having already accepted it. She knew her girl needed a man to take the edge off and the six foot black Adonis before them looked like he was just the one to end her drought.

Flustered, Kiyah turned her body completely so that she was facing the rude nigga with her hands placed firmly on her hips. She wasn't trying to spend her night running from his ass because he'd bought them drinks. Tonight was supposed to be all about her and her bestie kicking it since it had been so long since they'd gone out. Maine kept her locked away and it had only gotten worse since he'd proposed a few months ago.

Just from looking at Major, Kiyah could tell that he was exactly the type she tried to steer clear of, even though her body hummed with desire from his presence alone. He was dressed plainly in a white vneck with dark blue straight leg jeans. Simple enough but the fresh Red Bottom sneakers on his feet and the ice around his neck and wrist gave away that he was a hood nigga or very good at pretending to be; but his vibe alone let her know that he was authentic. Kiyah shook her head as he sized her up. She knew she looked damn good in fire red, tight fitting Yves Saint Laurent dress she wore. Her caramel skin was void of makeup besides the Fenty Stunna lip paint that covered her full lips. The thirty inch Brazilian sew-in she was rocking, courtesy of Mercedes, was laid and flowing down her back. She was putting half the women in there to shame and she wasn't even trying that hard.

"Well, *Major*... I appreciate the gesture, but I'm far from interested. Try your luck with her, she looks thirsty enough." Kiyah tilted her head and looked at the girl sitting behind him. Having heard what she said, the girl's eyes widened in shock as Major also looked her way. Before he could even bring his attention back to her, Kiyah had grabbed Mercedes' hand and her drink and was plowing through the crowd.

"Now why you do him like that friend? You know you need some, and it ain't like he was ugly." Mercedes teased, causing Kiyah to roll her eyes.

"Bitch ain't nobody studying his black ass, and I damn sure don't need none. I get enough dick." Kiyah lied. Even though she didn't want to admit it, she was definitely attracted to Major, sexually anyway, and that more than likely had everything to do with the fact that she had been without any good sex in ...... awhile.

"Keep tellin' yourself that." Mercedes chuckled and finished off her drink.

"Whatever... fuck all that! I'm tryna finish getting fucked up and dancing cause ain't no telling when Maine gone let you back out the house!" Kiyah drank the rest of the Long Island that was in her glass and sat it on the small table before pulling Mercedes to her feet. She could tell that the mention of her bestie's man put a damper on her mood just that quick, but a few more drinks would cure that.

Hours later after the two women had gone way past their drinking limit, Mercedes tried her best to tiptoe into the house. It was completely pitch black inside and she figured that for sure Maine was dead asleep, and she wouldn't have to worry about the bitch fit he was going to throw until the morning. Feeling confident that she was in the clear, she made her way up the stairs, trying to be as quiet as possible. First, she checked on their two year old son Baby J. He was sound asleep in his little Ninja Turtle toddler bed, snoring like a grown ass man. A giggle bubbled in her throat at how loud he was, and she slapped a hand over her mouth to quiet herself. The last thing she wanted to do was wake Jermaine up, especially when she was so drunk that she wouldn't even be able to fight back. When she finally composed herself, Mercedes closed the door and continued up the hall to her bedroom.

"Where the fuck you been?" Maine's deep baritone filled the dark room as soon as she stepped inside. She wasn't expecting that and she felled into the wall behind her. Fear invaded her body as he switched on the light and stormed over with his face full of rage. Mercedes was so caught off guard that she hadn't thought of any excuse as to why she had been gone so long.

"I-I....um..."

"You don't even gotta answer that! You had to be out thottin' in this lil ass dress!" He roared and sent a fist into her face. Upon impact, Mercedes saw stars and her hands immediately went up to block the blows that he began to rain down on her body. Within seconds, she was on the floor, but Maine wasn't finished yet. He paused briefly, giving her just enough time to pull herself up against the wall, but he returned just that fast, ripping the thin fabric from her body. If he wasn't mad before, he was even more enraged at the sight of the thong she was wearing. With a deranged grunt, he snatched her head back and sent another barrage of punches to her head and face. Mercedes wondered how she had gotten into such a dangerous situation. Three years ago when she'd met Maine, he seemed so charming and sweet. Coming from a home where the compliments and the love were nonexistent had her jumping head first into a relationship with him, and she'd quickly gotten pregnant; although at times, she wondered if that had been a trap within itself. It seemed like as soon as she had gotten pregnant with their son, he became overly possessive. Often demanding to know where she was and who she was with, to the point that she just stopped going anywhere to avoid the accusations of infi-

TORN BETWEEN BAE AND THE THUG NEXT DOOR

delity. Maine had never raised a hand to her; although, he occasionally would grab her by the neck or push her, those small instances turning into slaps and punches damn near as soon as she had Baby J. Flash forward to the present and there wasn't a day that went by it seemed that he wasn't beating her for one reason or another. She could barely breathe without it being too loud for him.

That day when he'd allowed her out to have a celebratory dinner with her best friend, she'd jumped at the chance and foolishly allowed herself to be swept up in the moment. A night of freedom from his constant demands and abuse felt like it was worth whatever hell he planned on inflicting. Now she was regretting those thoughts. With blood flowing from her nose and into her mouth, she did her best not to scream. Maine hated for their son to see him putting his hands on her, and if by chance Baby J heard the commotion and came in search of his mother, the beatings were that much worse.

Unsatisfied with the amount of damage he'd done, Maine stood up and pulled the belt from his jeans as Mercedes laid there moaning.

"Shut up bitch before you wake my son up! Yo hoe ass wasn't crying when you was out there lookin' like a thot with Kiyah was you!" The ringing in her ears made it sound as if he was miles away, but as soon as she felt the first lick of his thick belt, she knew he was right there with her still. "Don't. Take. Yo. Dumb. Ass. Back. Out. This. House! No! More!" He barked, hitting her between every word like she was a little ass kid getting spanked. Mercedes laid there unable to even fight back, even though it would have been pointless because she was no match for him.

After letting out his frustrations on her, Maine went around the room knocking over lamps and all of the shit she had on their dresser. "Get yo dumb ass off the floor! You ain't that hurt and clean this fuckin' room up!"

With that, he stepped over her battered body and out of the room coolly like he hadn't just beaten her like a man. Instinctively, Mercedes dragged herself up as pain coursed through every part of her body and staggered to her feet. Despite having drank so many shots she couldn't count, she still felt every single punch and welt she had on her body and she was damn sure sober. The sight of her bright red and swollen

<5</5>

legs brought on another round of tears. She had done so good hiding the bruises and black eyes with makeup that she was a pro in her own right, but there was no amount of foundation or concealer that she could use to cover the recent shit up, not after he'd destroyed everything that sat on the dresser.

Dizziness hit her as soon as she tried to take a step, and she stopped briefly to try and gain her composure. Barely being able to see out of her blood stained eye, she fumbled to the bathroom. The sight of her once blemish free golden skin had tears once again stinging her eyes. That nigga had dragged her so low. Her self esteem was already low, but with Jermaine, it had taken a straight nose dive to nonexistent. Messing with him, she'd had to get two teeth replaced already and had a thinning spot in the back of her head that she always had to cover because he'd pulled it so many times. Shaking her head at the mess she'd gotten herself into, she grabbed one of their plush red and golden face towels off of the rack and began to clean herself up. Once all of the blood was gone, she could see that despite a red swollen nose, a busted lip, and a black eye, the damage wasn't as bad as she thought. Mercedes laughed bitterly at how dumb that sounded and went to work on her sore legs. She knew that she wouldn't be able to face her best friend for a long time since she was sure Jermaine would lock her up until further notice. It wasn't like she had a job or anything to go to since he'd scooped her up fresh out of high school. Besides taking care of their son, the only skills she had was doing hair and make-up since she was constantly having to cover up his many beatings over the years. With a heavy sigh, she grabbed a couple of ibuprofen from the bottle that they kept on hand and swallowed them dry before heading into the bedroom so that she could further clean up her fiancé's mess. There wasn't anywhere for her to go that he wouldn't find her, and she had long resigned herself to the fact that she was stuck with him for life. He always told her that it was *until death do us part* and she knew that he would make good on that promise if she ever tried to leave.

❧ 2 ❧

Kiyah stretched in her queen size bed and finally rolled over when her alarm sounded a few minutes later. Saturday was normally the only day that she slept past nine, but since Mercedes was doing her makeup, she had to get up. Kiyah's hair would need to be flat ironed again since she sweated it out the night before; she was sure Mercedes wouldn't mind doing that too. Kiyah was good at a lot of shit, but hair wasn't it and she had no problem admitting it. Her birthday celebrations were continuing that night, so she needed to get a move on. She grabbed her phone and made her way to the bathroom to handle her hygiene. It felt so good to be out with her bestie the night before, and she hoped that she could talk her into hanging out again because she truly deserved a break.

After Kiyah relieved her bladder and scrolled through social media for a few minutes, she turned the shower on and stepped in once the water was good and hot. The water cascaded down Kiyah's body and she relaxed. For a brief moment, she thought about *him*, but quickly shrugged those thoughts to the side. Kiyah couldn't even remember his name, but his smooth chocolate skin was a turn on like no other. Just by looking at him, she knew that he was into the street life and Kiyah avoided those type of men at all costs. She washed and rinsed off two times and then got out and dried off with her plush lavender towel that was hanging on the rack.

Twenty minutes later, Kiyah was dressed in a black and white PINK jogger with a pair of Vapormax. Kiyah was a sucker for sneakers; buying them was her guilty pleasure. She had her eyes set on a new pair that she told herself would be her graduation gift to herself in a couple of months. After obtaining her Bachelor's a couple of years ago, Kiyah jumped straight into a Master's program for Business Management and Consulting. Working for herself was always the goal, but Kiyah knew that she needed a lot of more money or the right connections to make that happen. She worked on campus in the business department and also part time at Foot Locker. It was safe to say that her part time check went straight back to her job, but she didn't care.

On the way to Mercedes' house, Kiyah called to see if she wanted anything to eat, but she didn't answer. She whipped into Chick-fil-A and grabbed something for herself, her Godson, and Mercedes. After paying and retrieving the bags, a dinging sound alerted Kiyah. When she looked at the dashboard, she saw that it was her gas light that made the sound. Pumping gas was always a drag and she always avoided it, but at that moment, she had no choice but to stop by the Quick Trip that was right next door. She parked at pump five and pulled her chicken biscuit out of the bag and put grape jelly on it before getting out. It wasn't her intent to eat it, but it was smelling too good to resist.

Kiyah noticed a car behind her waiting and wondered why the asshole didn't go to one of the empty pumps instead of getting behind her. She hurriedly finished her food and then got out and threw her trash away. Kiyah grabbed her debit card from her wallet and inserted it at the pump.

"Well this must be fate," a voice startled her.

Kiyah turned around and locked eyes with the same man from the night before.

"You stalking me?" she quipped.

"Chill ma, that ain't even my type... but it's good to see you again so soon since you played a nigga to the left last night," he coolly replied.

"Major," Kiyah said out loud, but really she only wanted to say it in her head. Just seeing him again made her remember his name.

"The one and only... and I know you're Miss Feisty Kiyah."

She rolled her eyes knowing that it wasn't anybody except Mercedes that had to have given him her name. Major grabbed the handle and pumped her gas before she had the chance to do it, not that she was complaining at all. If Kiyah was a self-conscious chick, she would be embarrassed by the way that Major was eye fucking her as he pumped the gas, but she just stared right back.

"You shouldn't let your car get this low on gas... but no worries, it'll be my responsibility from here on out."

"You really cocky for real huh."

"Confident baby... I'm never cocky, always confident," he smiled, displaying a perfect set of pearly whites that made Kiyah's pussy tingle.

"Well... thank you so much Mr. Major... I really appreciate this kind gesture but..."

"You're interested. Don't lie to yourself... but check this shit out, next time I see you, it won't be no games. If I wasn't headed to a meeting, we would go on our first date. But I'ma let you slide for now," he told her and walked away.

Kiyah stood there for a moment lost in her own thoughts. She couldn't believe the effect that Major had on her. She locked eyes with him and he smiled at her again. Kiyah gathered herself and then got in her white Honda Accord and left the gas station. She couldn't lie, Major was on her mind for the remainder of the seven minutes it took for her to get to Mercedes' crib. Not bothering to call or text, Kiyah grabbed the food, along with her phone and got out.

"Get in the kitchen and get my son some fuckin' food... be a better mother instead of a thot," Maine's voice boomed right as Kiyah was about to knock on the door.

To her surprise, the door was cracked, so she took it upon herself to go on inside. Her friend rounded the corner and Kiyah instantly noticed the bruises on her face. Since she only had on a pair of shorts, she even saw bruises all over her legs. Kiyah knew that Maine was controlling, but she didn't think that he would ever put his hands on

Mercedes. She dropped the bag with the food and rushed Maine like she was a nigga.

"Motherfucker, you beat my friend... you a pussy ass nigga!" Kiyah caught Maine off guard and punched him repeatedly, making him fall over onto the couch.

"Kiyah noooo!" Mercedes screamed and pulled her away.

"Get the fuck outta my house!" Maine boomed.

"Nigga, I ain't goin' nowhere!" Kiyah based.

She looked at her friend and saw the timid look on her face. She had never witnessed such fear so up close and personal in her life. Kiyah couldn't imagine leaving her friend, but she also didn't want to cause any extra harm to her. She knew that she had to think fast.

"It's okay Kiyah... just leave," Mercedes whimpered.

Kiyah looked at her like she was crazy.

"I'm not leaving my friend. I'll be gone when you get back though asshole," she hissed at Maine.

"She better be gone when I get back," Maine eyed Mercedes and left.

As soon as he was gone, Mercedes broke down crying and Kiyah pulled her in for a hug and cried with her.

3

Duke awoke to the sound of his alarm and let out an aggravated grunt. After making the big move down to Atlanta the day before, he was already tired but listening to an hour or so of his new neighbors fighting made him miss out on his much needed sleep. It sounded like the nigga was over there killing his bitch. Off instinct, he was ready to walk across the yard and beat dude's ass, but he had to remind himself that it wasn't his business. He'd just moved back after ten years and it wasn't time to play captain save-a-hoe. The only thing that he needed to worry about was the promotion he was about to receive and how much money came along with that. Still, he fully intended on letting them know to keep that shit down next time as soon as he saw them.

He got out of bed and silently cursed himself for not paying attention to how close his house was to theirs that he could even hear what the fuck they had going on over there. Theirs had to have been the closest houses in the whole neighborhood if nobody else heard that shit and hadn't called the police. If he would have known that was the type of shit he'd be dealing with, he should have just moved to the hood. Duke shut off the still beeping alarm and tried to put the whole situation to the back of his mind as he prepared himself for the meeting he was scheduled to attend in the next couple hours.

After brushing his teeth and taking a shower, he stepped inside of the walk-in closet that was big enough to be a room itself. Not really feeling the need to impress anybody, he threw on a pair of black jeans, a white wife beater, and his Nike hoodie that matched the color of his Space Jam Jordan's perfectly. With his Miami Cuban draped on his neck and a Bulgari Octo strapped to his wrist, he was all set.

The minute he rounded the corner into the kitchen, he was greeted by his little sister Dreka, who was in the process of fucking up breakfast.

"Heyyyy Dookie!" She cheesed excitedly, calling him by the nickname she'd given him years ago. A frown immediately covered Duke's face because he hated when she called him that.

"Aye quit fuckin' calling me that childish shit Dreka fore I go upside yo head." He threatened.

"You always say that, and don't shit ever happen. I'm gone call you Dookie til the day I die!" She stuck her tongue out and cracked another egg into the bowl that sat in front of her. Dreka was eighteen going on eight, but she was the only person on the earth that he cared about. Ever since their mama passed five years before, it had been just the two of them, and he made it his mission to provide for her. She'd recently graduated from high school, and he was trying to talk her stubborn ass into going to college; but she claimed that she wanted to take a year off from school like she was some white kid. Duke had laid off on pressuring her but in due time, she was going to be taking her ass to somebody's school.

"If you try and eat the shit you mixing in that bowl, today gone be the last day you call anybody anything. You don't see them fuckin' shells in there?" He frowned at how many egg shells and shit were floating around with the yolks. That was exactly the reason why he always cooked or ordered out. He had made the mistake of eating some shit she'd made one time, and he regretted it almost as soon as it touched his stomach.

"Duh, I was gone pick them out! Ain't you got somewhere you

need to go today? Carry your worrisome ass on!" She snapped, causing Duke to look down at his watch. At that point, he had about an hour to make it to his destination so he would have to postpone the trip to IHOP he had planned on making.

"You right, I gotta dip but throw that shit out and just buy you something." He tossed a couple hundred dollar bills onto the island and turned to leave, ignoring whatever smart ass comment her ass had to say. Despite all of the shit he had talked, he still found himself looking across the way at the house next door and noticing how still it was. He could imagine that after the way them muthafuckas was fighting, they'd still be asleep. *Lucky them.* Duke shook his bitter thoughts away and tried to get focused on the move he was about to make. Thanks to his homie Major, he was about to be running shit and stepping on toes, which he didn't mind at all. He was actually looking forward to the looks on them niggas faces when they were told that a new nigga was going to be taking over.

⚜

"WHAT THE FUCK YOU MEAN THIS NIGGA IN CHARGE?!"

Duke squinted his eyes at the dude that he now knew as Maine. Even before anything had been said in the meeting, he was mean mugging and looking like he smelled shit. He could admit that he would be salty too if a new nigga was coming in and telling him what to do, but he would've been smart enough not to let the shit show. Maine was so mad, you could damn near see steam coming out of his ears. Major went to answer his question, but Duke stopped him with a tap on the arm.

"I got it." He leaned on the table and pinned Maine down with a stare as he addressed the whole room. "This gone be the first *and* last time I discuss this shit with you niggas. From now on, I'm in charge, I'm running this shit! If you got any issues with it, I don't mind letting my gun talk for me! Any further questions?" He smirked as Maine sat back in his seat like a scolded child and kept his mouth shut just like everybody else in the room.

"Well, since that's all figured out, you niggas are dismissed." Major stood back grinning proudly at the way his childhood friend had handled the situation. He knew he had made a good decision when it came to making Duke the next in line as opposed to his current workers, especially Maine. "Aye Maine!" He called him back before he could make it fully out of the room. "I fucks with you, but don't *ever* fuckin' question me again!"

Duke enjoyed the way that Maine's face crumbled after getting reprimanded before storming out of the room behind everybody else. He wasn't the type that went around just starting problems with niggas, but something about Maine rubbed him the wrong way, giving Duke a bad vibe. He questioned how Major didn't see it, but knew that with his presence around, he was bound to.

"Yo ass already got niggas tight!" Major laughed and slapped hands with Duke as soon as the room was empty. Not able to hide his grin, Duke shrugged.

"Shiiit, that's on them. I don't need none of they ass to be my friend. I'm just tryna get to the money."

"Real shit. How was the move tho and how Dreka's lil young ass doin'?" Major asked as they walked out of the warehouse and to their cars.

"Dreka good but nigga, I'm in the wrong neighborhood! Them mutha fuckas next door was fighting loud as hell nigga! I need to be out where you at! North Bankhead got ghetto neighbors just like the hood!" He laughed even though he was still irritated by the inconvenience.

"Nah that's a good spot, you just live next to the wrong mutha fuckas! Shiiit, Maine's ass live out that way too I think."

"Ah hell nah... that just dropped the property value fasho!" They shared a laugh.

"For real, Maine straight man... he just fucked up about the change, but he ain't gone be a problem." Major said. Duke could understand that Major fucked with Maine to an extent, so he wasn't going to bad mouth him; but, his gut told him that nigga was a clown.

"Shit for his sake, I hope not."

"You a fool, but let me get up outta here. I'm gone hit you up with the details about the next shipment." Major shook his head as he opened up the door to his bad ass red Mercedes AMG.

"Bet." Duke nodded and got into his own Maserati and pulled off, ready to grab something else to eat and go home to catch up on his sleep.

4

Major left the meeting feeling pretty good about the direction in which things were going for him and his crew. He knew that Maine would probably feel some type of way about not being promoted, but he felt like he would be okay in no time. Duke seemed to think differently, but Major had faith in Maine because they both knew that he was distracted at times and never said why. Major had to make the decision that he felt was best and that was exactly what he did. He went to his downtown office and checked on his investments for the next hour and a half and then closed his MacBook Pro once he was satisfied. If it wasn't for his ex, Nisha, he wouldn't have been up on technology. She spent up a lot of his money, but she also kept him up on game and for that, he had to appreciate her.

After gathering his few belongings, Major prepared for his exit. He secured his strap out of habit and made his way to the elevator. As soon as he made it to the parking garage, his phone vibrated in his pocket, but he ignored it when he saw someone standing next to his car. Major felt like his eyes must have been playing tricks on him, but the closer he got, he knew they weren't.

"Maine? What you doin' down here bruh?"

"I came to take care of some business, but then figured I'd wait around and holla at you."

"What's up?" he quizzed.

"It ain't that I'm questioning you, but I just need to know man to man, why you overlooked me for the promotion after all the work I done put in?"

"Maine... it's mighty funny that you start a sentence saying you ain't questioning me but then question me. You know me and I normally wouldn't take that kinda disrespect, but because we have so much history and I love you like a brother, I'ma give you that. Now the reason I chose Duke is simple... we got more than history than me and you, and he don't let distractions fuck up the job," Major stated, referring to a couple of fuck ups that were caused by Maine.

"Ain't no hate or no shit man, I just wanted to hear from you. But you need to let ol' boy know I ain't no punk."

"We all on the same team, making the same money... In no time, you know I'll be completely done, and it'll just be y'all two, so I hope you a man of your word," Major sternly stated.

"It's all good bruh," Maine dapped him up and then walked away.

Major got in his car and Duke's words rang in his head again. He hoped that Maine didn't flip and start any bullshit. The nigga was still eating good, but Major was smart enough to know that pride was a motherfucker. As soon as Major crunk up and put his car in reverse, his phone vibrated again, so he pulled it out of his pocket. It was crazy that she was texting when he hadn't been too long got done thinking about her ass. Major shot a confirmation text back and then made his way towards his destination.

Thirty minutes later, Major was turning into Olive Garden by request. As soon as he got out and made his way in, he spotted her. What he wasn't prepared for was her protruding belly.

"Oh, I don't get no hug today?" Nisha smiled and wrapped her arms around him.

"What's goin' on?"

"Can we eat first pleeaasseee? We're starving," Nisha pouted.

The appetite that Major had was gone just that fast. He began mentally calculating shit in his head and knew that he hadn't slid up in

Kinisha raw in a long ass time. She hadn't ever really been on no bull-shit with him lately, but his thoughts were getting the best of him. Once they were seated, he didn't waste any time grilling her after the waitress took their drink and food orders since Nisha knew what she wanted.

"Yo Nisha, what the fuck?" he asked while pointing to her belly.

"Calm ya nerves... I didn't pop up to say this was your baby..."

Major released a breath that he didn't realize he was even holding after those words escaped Nisha's lips. They hadn't been in a relation-ship in a couple of years, but they did have sex months ago on some platonic type shit and that was what had Major worried. He didn't know if the rubber broke, if she stole some sperm, or what. Although Major would always have love for Nisha because of everything she helped him with, they could never be together because she had broken his trust one time and that was all took in a relationship with him.

"So who done got you knocked up?" he finally asked.

"Welllll.... Here's the thing, I really don't know who the father is."

"Fuck you mean? You out here like that now?" Major cringed.

"No nigga... I went to the sperm bank," Nisha whispered.

"Stop playing girl... who the daddy? Must be a lame," he chuckled.

When he saw that she wasn't smiling, Major's face got serious.

"You serious yo?"

"Yes. I'm older than you so ya know... I was ready to have a baby," she shrugged.

Nisha started telling him about how and why she went through the process, and Major listened attentively. He was in shock, but he respected her boldness at the same time. Nisha was ten years older than you so ya know she did it; but low-key, he wished that she would have did it the traditional way just to give the baby a family. Major's parents were still together after all these years and living the life. They lived in Cali as well as his sister, but Major took the opportu-nity to leave when his uncle presented it to him fresh out of high school. He was nine years in and looking to fully retire by his thirtieth birthday, which was four years away.

"Well no wonder yo ass been MIA," Major joked to lighten the mood.

"Yeeaahhh, I had to stay low-key," she shrugged.

The waitress brought their food and as soon as she left, the conversation shifted.

"Sooo do you have a special lady in your life yet?" Nisha queried.

"Yep," Major confidently answered while thinking about Kiyah.

"Okay, well spill it."

"Nah, ain't too much to tell yet, but just know I've found my wife," he winked.

Major thought he saw a hint of sadness on Nisha's face, but she quickly smiled and changed the subject to baby names and stuff. He could tell that having a baby made her happy and he was happy for her. They finished their meals and Major paid the check and left a tip. Once they made it to the front, Major couldn't believe his fuckin' eyes. There was no way in hell he was standing there staring at Kiyah.

5

Kiyah must have worried the shit out of Maine because ever since the day that she had come over, he'd been extremely sweet. In the back of her mind, Mercedes knew that it was just his same cycle repeating itself, but at the same time, she welcomed the affection. Almost every time that he put his hands on her, he would spend days, or in this case weeks, trying to make it up to her. Unfortunately, it always worked....at least until the next time he decided to take his frustrations out on her.

The little bit of reprieve was coming to an end though because it had been a few days since she'd received a gift or a compliment from him. That was a clear indication of Maine getting comfortable that she wasn't going to leave, so it was back to the regularly scheduled program. The only plus to this was that during the weeks of his groveling, he'd allowed her to schedule someone for a hair appointment outside of the house, and even better, he agreed to watch Baby J while she went.

Excitement coursed through her just at the thought of leaving the beautiful prison they resided in. She had been dressed and ready an hour before her baby woke up, that's just how thirsty she was.

"Hung gree!"

"I'm almost done lil man. You ready to spend the day with daddy?" Mercedes smiled at her son as she sliced up a couple strawberries to add onto his plate of eggs and sausage. He happily clapped his hands and nodded. It wasn't every day that he got to spend time with Maine, but whenever he did, he always enjoyed it. Mercedes could say a lot about him, but he was a damn good father. Sitting the plate down in front of him, she damn near jumped out of her skin at the sight of Maine standing behind her. He didn't say a word as he took her in from head to toe with narrowed eyes.

"H-Heyy baby... I uh... made breakfast. You hungry?" she asked in a high pitched tone filled with nervousness. She'd made sure to keep her make up very natural and light so as to only cover the fading bruises. Her outfit while cute wasn't anything form fitting or revealing. In fact, she had lost a few pounds recently; the gray Champion hoodie and jogger set fitted about a size too big. With the white Nike Shox that were on her small feet, she was dressed for comfort and fully prepared for the two hours it would take to do the girl Raina's hair.

"Fuck is you goin'?" he avoided her question and asked one of his own. It was obvious that he'd forgotten the conversation they'd had about her leaving, but he couldn't change his mind about her going... well she hoped he wouldn't.

"I have a client today, remember? You told me I could go, and that you'd keep Baby J." she tried to smile naturally as if she wasn't shivering inside. It was obvious that he didn't remember, or he didn't want to admit that he'd agreed to it. Instead, he did the next best thing. Sabotage.

"I can't watch lil dude today, I got some important shit to do." He dismissed her, turning his back and snagging one of the sausages off of the pan she had nearby.

"But... you promised... you know I can't have him running around while I'm working--"

"And I can't have his ass with me while I'm out here in the streets! Them bitches that pay you for them kitchen do's don't give a fuck if he there! You acting like that shit a real job, yo ass lucky I'm even letting you out after that shit you pulled with Kiyah. I shouldn't let yo ass go nowhere!" Mercedes jumped back at the outburst, afraid of what he might do. The way that his face contorted made him almost unrecognizable to her. Maine wasn't an ugly nigga by far. He was the color of milk chocolate with a full beard and deep waves. You would never think as attractive as he was that he was such a damn lunatic though. Fearful that he would snatch away her freedom, she quickly relented. She'd rather be able to go outside with Baby J than to endure another day in the house with him.

"Okay, I'll take him with me."

"Good, make me a plate before you go." He smirked before sitting down and finally engaging their son.

◊

HOURS LATER, MERCEDES WAS FINALLY DONE WITH THE SEW-IN AND lace frontal that Raina had wanted, despite Baby J being there. She'd been so happy with the way that it had turned out that she'd asked for Mercedes' social media and some business cards to put her friends on. Flattered, Mercedes gave her the name for both her Facebook and Instagram before snapping a few pictures to add to her pages. She hoped that eventually Maine would see the small buzz she was getting and allow her to go to school and maybe work at a shop. As it stood, all he did was talk shit about what she did like she wasn't talented, even though she had more than a few women that could vouch for her. He still thought that she was doing these hairstyles for fifty dollars when she wasn't accepting anything less than two hundred for her services. So far on the list of fuck boy tendencies, he hadn't added taking her money to the many things that he did, but she didn't believe that he would allow her to make too much money on her own. She may have been dumb about some things but knew to keep her a "secret stash."

After getting her duffle and everything else into the car, she pulled off with a growling stomach. Maine, who had been texting her the entire time that she'd been gone, was now still stalking her line since she told him she was leaving. With a roll of her eyes, she pulled into Five Guys since she had a taste for a greasy burger. She'd thought that maybe she would have time to take Baby J to the park before his nap, but it was clear that Maine wanted her home asap.

Mercedes parked carefully next to a Maserati and hurried to let Maine know that she was stopping to grab some food and she would be right home. She made sure to ask if he wanted anything as she eased out of the car since the parking spot was so tight. She couldn't help but be irritated as she went to help Baby J out too. Like what type of person with a car that expensive would take up damn near two spaces to park. With a sigh, she strutted inside with her baby on her hip and got in line just as Maine responded with his food order.

As usual, the place was packed and she dreaded standing in the long ass line, but she was too far to turn back now. Plus the smell of the food had her stomach growling harder.

"I want fwies ma!" Baby J patted her shoulder and said.

"Okay but I'm getting you a burger too. Yo lil greedy butt ain't bouta be just eating mine."

"Fwies!"

Mercedes chuckled at how his little eyebrows drew together; he looked just like his daddy, but where it was cute on him, the same angry face would bring fear coming from Maine. The line grew shorter and shorter as they continued to argue about him getting a burger too.

"Aye who the fuck out here in this silver Honda!" the angry voice called out from behind her over all the noise in the crowded restaurant. It seemed like everybody got quiet as hell all of a sudden, and despite fearing the confrontation, Mercedes turned around, knowing that it was the owner of the Maserati and he was talking about her old 2010 Honda Civic. Her breath caught in her throat when she laid eyes on the fine ass caramel skinned brother standing in front of the door with an angry scowl. He was tall as hell with a medium build, and she instantly pictured herself being held in his arms as he death stroked her.

"Um... it's- I'm driving the Honda." Mercedes finally said after finding her voice. The guy looked around, trying to find the tiny voice out of the crowd of people. When his eyes finally landed on hers, his expression softened up but only for a second.

"Come move that shit, I ain't tryna be here all day!" Despite the fact that he didn't crack a smile, Mercedes still found herself chuckling lightly. There was no way he seriously thought she was about to get out of line just to move her car when he was the one who had parked fucked up.

"I'm literally in line right now. Can I at least order my food first?" she scoffed in disbelief.

"No." he said with a shrug. "I obviously parked in a way that would stop a muhfucka from parking next to me. Out of everybody in here, yo ass decided to do the exact opposite so now, you gotta come move so I don't scratch my shit up tryna get out." He didn't raise his voice at all, but the authority behind it spoke volumes. Mercedes looked around for anyone of the many men in the building to say something in her defense, but they all were avoiding eye contact, which garnered a cocky grin from him. Entirely over the situation and the man himself, she sighed heavily.

"Fine." She grumbled, fighting back tears as she stormed around the people standing there and out of the door. That wasn't the first time that she'd had to jump when a man told her to, but it damn sure brought on the same feelings of anger and hurt. It seemed like there was a vibe that she gave off that showed how weak she was and there wasn't shit that she could do about it. Hell, that nigga hadn't even cared that she had her son with her. Mercedes knew that if it had been Kiyah, she would have raised hell before she ever went to move her car, but not her. The situation just continued to show her just how pathetic she was. With blurred vision, she strapped Baby J into his car seat, and then went around to her side with the guy standing back to make sure she didn't scratch his car. *Asshole!* She couldn't help thinking as she backed up, preparing to have Uber Eats bring them food.

"Mama, I want fwies!" Baby J hollered from the backseat, sounding like he was about to cry too. She thought about hitting the nigga's cocky ass but decided against it when she considered going to jail for murder.

"I know baby, we just gone have them deliver okay." She reassured him as she turned out of the parking lot and headed home. The fifteen minute drive gave her a few minutes to get herself together before she had to deal with Maine's worrisome ass. He would for sure want to know what had taken her so long when she didn't even have the food, but she would just tell him that the wait was too long. Turned out that she didn't even need the excuse because for all the rushing that he'd done, Jermaine's damn car wasn't even in the driveway when she pulled up. Sadly, she didn't even have the energy to be upset.

❧ 6 ❧

"See, I told you this nigga was gone try me." Duke fumed as he
paced the confines of Major's home office. The very first pick
up that he'd had scheduled with Maine's bitch ass was fucked
up cause he didn't show. Every other person who was supposed to get
their shit came on the day and time that had been given except for
that nigga and he was more than pissed.

"Look man, calm down ayite. Maine not the type to skip out on a
pick up. It was probably his girl or his son." Major shrugged, causing
Duke to look at him crazy. Duke could understand that he didn't have
a reason to doubt the things that he was saying about the dude. Hell,
he'd known him way longer than Duke had, but in his mind, any nigga
that would pull some hoe shit just because a nigga was in charge was
suspect. He hadn't given Maine any reason to buck at all, but for some
reason, he was trying to see how far he could go. What Maine failed to
realize was that Major was only there to advise him before he took
over. Whatever love that nigga had for him wouldn't mean shit if it got
in the way of his money.

"That nigga knew what the fuck he was doin'." Duke scoffed

"Let's just hear what his ass gotta say before we jump to conclu-
sions ayite. I been workin' with Maine for years man and it ain't never

26

been no serious issues. He makes me good money, which means he'll make *you* good money. If we can resolve whatever this issue is without losing a good worker, then that's all I'm worried bout. And once you're completely in my position, that's all you gone be worried bout too." A knock at the door paused the debate the two men were having and Major's maid Gloria stepped in.

"Your guest." She said simply, standing off to the side as Maine walked in casually like he hadn't done shit. Gloria left right back out and Duke set his dark gaze on Maine.

"Fuck was you at today nigga?" he asked before Maine had a chance to sit down.

"Calm down Duke."

"Yeah, calm yo ass down boy." Maine added tauntingly.

"You sounding real casual for a nigga who missed out on some money today." Major finally addressed him, causing the grin to slip from his face. "Please tell me that what happened was due to an emergency and not yo ego my nigga. I know it ain't no way you letting a promotion stop you from taking care of yo seed...right?"

"Mannnnn... ain't nobody pressed bout that, my shorty had something to do and couldn't take my son, and I damn sure ain't bringing him to no shit like that, so I didn't go." He shrugged, avoiding eye contact, a clear indication of deceit.

"And you couldn't let a muhfucka know so I wouldn't be sittin' there waitin' on you for nothin?" Duke jumped in.

"Fuck I look like nigga, I ain't gotta check in with you. You shoulda knew what it was when I ain't show up." Maine spat, sizing Duke up.

"Nigga, you look like *you* work for *me*, so you *do* gotta check in. Matter fact, yo ass *done* with weight, I'm puttin' you at the trap!"

"Hell nah! I ain't fuckin' baggin' or sellin' shit! I got niggas doin' that type of shit for me!" Maine's face balled up instantly. He looked to Major for help, but that nigga just shrugged.

"Looks like you are or your ass ain't getting no money." Duke laughed sinisterly. "Better get there early, you know the trap never sleeps." He tossed out over his shoulder as he left the room. There wasn't anything else that needed to be said on his part. If Maine knew what was good for him, he would be his ass there.

Duke swaggered to his car feeling a little better since he had gotten to address the shit. He hated for his time to be wasted, and when he sat at the warehouse for an hour past the time he was supposed to, he was beyond mad. The shit had him so heated that he took out his frustrations on anybody who he ran across that day. He still felt a little bad about the way that he had handled shorty in the restaurant. It wasn't like him to be that rude and damn sure not towards a female, especially one as fine as her. Once he'd calmed down some, he realized that he had went too damn hard on her and felt bad as fuck. It wasn't shit he could do about it now though, so it wasn't no point in dwelling on it. Besides that, Atlanta was so damn big, there was probably no chance he'd see her fine ass again; but if he did, he was for sure gone come at her different. The thought of her pretty ass face and thick body that she tried to hide behind them sweats had him bricking up, and he instantly grabbed his phone and texted this little bitch Raina that he'd reconnected with. They went to high school together and she was the first familiar face that he'd come across since he'd moved back besides Major. Her ass was looking too good when he saw her at the mall a week ago, but after getting her number, he hadn't had time to fuck with her. Tonight was gone be her lucky night though because he needed a freak of her caliber to take his mind off shorty in the gray.

❦

NOT EVEN AN HOUR LATER, DUKE WAS PULLING UP TO THE HOTEL they'd agreed to meet at. He wanted to fuck, but he wasn't about to meet her at her crib without knowing shit about her besides that her ass was fat. As soon as he hit the door, Raina was all over him, trying to kiss and suck on his neck.

"Nah, handle this shit first." He ordered, grabbing his semi hard dick. Kissing and all that shit wasn't on the menu, and when she immediately dropped down to her knees and released his dick with no questions asked, he knew she was just what he needed.

"Mmmmm mm." she moaned as his dick touched the back of her throat. She stared up at him with wide eyes, and he grabbed a handful of her hair in his hand, guiding himself further into her mouth. Trying to keep up, she used two hands like she was working a pepper grinder and let slob dribble out of her mouth and down her chest. It was some of the sloppiest head he'd ever gotten, and before he knew it, he was sending his kids to rest in her stomach. Shorty swallowed every drop and licked her lips like she wanted more. Like every dick eating bitch that he knew, Raina jumped to her feet, obviously happy with her skills.

"Can we at least get on the bed now? My knees hurt Duke." She whined then flipped her hair. "And don't grab my hair no more. I just got this shit done and it still kinda hurt."

"Is you bouta fuck or not, cause all that other shit ain't my concern?" he questioned, prepared to either get undressed or stuff his dick back into his jeans. Although, if he had to do the latter, he'd be ready to strangle Raina's ass for wasting his time. The indifference in his voice must have alarmed her, desperation was evident on her face as she slipped off the black tights and crop top, making her entire body visible.

"I'm definitely about to fuck." She purred, pulling him with her to the bed. It was obvious that she had taken in his clothes, car, and the way that he looked to mean that he was a come up. Little did she know, it wouldn't be that easy to pin him down. Duke was going to do what he wanted when he wanted. He grabbed a condom out of his pocket before he let his pants hit the floor and stretched it over his dick while Raina laid down on her back in front of him, playing in her pussy. Besides the sound of her moans filling the room, the only other thing that could be heard was her fingers slipping in and out of her wetness. She moved her body close to the edge and raised her hips. "Come taste it...."

Instead of replying to the nonsense she was talking, Duke flipped her over so that she was propped up on her knees with her ass tooted in the air. Rubbing his tip through the puddle in her center, he barely gave her time to prepare before he plunged inside her. Off top, Duke noticed two things: one was that Raina barely had any walls, and two, his nut was gone be a struggle to get.

"Ooooh, shit you so fuckin' big!" she panted as he dug deep into her guts. *Not big enough.* He thought. Her voice was annoying the fuck out of him; he tried to tune her out by thinking of shorty from Five Guys. With his eyes closed tight, he pushed her fully down into the mattress. Imagining that the cries of pleasure were coming from ole girl had his nut ready to spill, and he pulled out and snatched the condom off, ejaculating onto her back. Duke couldn't help but to be surprised at how strong that nut had been just from thinking about a bitch whose name he didn't even know. Without waiting for Raina to get her lazy ass up, he made his way to the bathroom to discard of the condom and clean his dick before he left. It took him all of five seconds in the bathroom, and he came straight out and pulled on his pants, ready to leave.

"You ain't bring me a towel?" she lifted her head, just enough to see that he was already putting his clothes on. "Tsk, you not even gone stay?" she asked while sitting up and looking at him expectantly, but he ain't have shit for her but the drying nut on her back.

"No, fuck I'ma stay here for when I got my own house?" He sneered at how stupid she sounded. "I'ma hit you up." Not even waiting for a reply, he opened the door and stepped out good and tired from the day's events and the two nuts he'd busted.

❦ 7 ❧

Kiyah grabbed her backpack, phone, car keys, and headed out. She had an exam in Microeconomics the following week and had a study date. After glancing at the time and noticing that she had some time to spare, Kiyah made a pit stop by Starbucks and ordered a Caramel Frappuccino with extra drizzle. After paying and retrieving her iced coffee, Kiyah headed towards downtown. She was sure that Chris was already there; he was the type who considered an hour early as on time. They were meeting at one of the cafés that was near where Chris' dad worked, but Kiyah had to have her coffee from one place.

Thirty minutes later, she was parking in a space that was too good to be true. Kiyah grabbed some change for the meter and then got out of her car. After paying for a few hours, she made her way inside and spotted Chris in a booth near the back. As soon as she made it to him, he stood up and gave her a hug.

"Hey Chris... how are you?"

"I'm just peachy," Chris replied and Kiyah chuckled.

Chris was the definition of lame, but he was very sweet and super smart. Kiyah knew that he probably had a little crush on her, but she was honest with him by letting him know that she wasn't interested in anything beyond studying. A waitress walked over and greeted the two of them and then took their orders. Kiyah really was content with the coffee she had, but Chris ordered an orange juice, turkey bacon, egg whites, and wheat toast.

"You even eat like a nerd," Kiyah teased him when the waitress left.

"If you fuel your body with great things, great things will come out," Chris boasted.

"Okaaayyyy... so you ready to get started? I feel confident today," Kiyah asserted.

"Ready as can be," Chris confirmed and pulled out a deck of flashcards.

"A group of buyers and sellers of a good or service and the institution..."

"Market," Kiyah cut him off.

"Analysis that involves comparing marginal benefits and..."

"Marginal Analysis," she cut him off and answered correctly again.

He went through half of the deck and Kiyah answered everything correctly.

"Okay I got one more for you and then we can switch to the other section..."

"The highest valued alternative that must be given up to engage in an activity."

"Opportunity cost... and I won't let this opportunity pass me by," Kiyah heard from behind her.

His voice sent chills down her spine. The last time she saw him, he was leaving Olive Garden with a pregnant woman who she assumed was his woman. Major tried to explain something to her, but Kiyah wasn't hearing it. His voice was sexy as hell, but she had to stay strong and steer clear of him.

"So you a real life stalker for real for real huh? Shouldn't you be somewhere with your little family?" Kiyah sassed.

"Aye partner, Ion mean no harm, but I'm taking over this date," Major addressed Chris.

"Umm, no you're not. Don't leave Chris," Kiyah affirmed once she saw Chris getting up.

Major gave Chris a look, and he hurriedly scrambled up.

"Leave the notes man... I'll make sure she gets an A," Major patted him on the back.

As soon as Chris got up, Major plopped into his seat like he belonged there. Kiyah wanted to be mad at his ass, but the weird feelings she had about him began to resurface. She didn't know why she was so drawn to him. Normally, Kiyah could shake a nigga off in a heartbeat, especially one she didn't even know; but deep down, she was intrigued by Mr. Major.

"How did you know the answer to that question?" she broke the silence amongst the two of them.

"I'm a jack of all trades baby... in time, you'll see it firsthand."

"Coc... I mean confident much?" she smiled.

"See, you're already learning me. Now let's get these questions outta the way so we can get to know each other."

Major asked Kiyah a series of questions and she answered each of them correctly. She was surprised by how comfortable she felt around him. They moved on to the next two sections with ease, and it was safe to say that she knew her shit. Two hours later, they were ordering some food and Kiyah stood to go to the restroom.

"Aye, don't dip out on me," he grabbed her hand and kissed it.

Kiyah smiled back and walked away. His touch and charm had her panties moist. While on the way to the bathroom, Kiyah could have sworn she saw Chris peeking from the corner, but someone bumped into her, and when she looked again, he was gone. She relieved her bladder, washed her hands, and sent Mercedes a quick text before exiting the bathroom. Kiyah felt so bad for her friend. Her heart broke into pieces a couple of weeks ago while listening to Mercedes justify why she had to stay with Maine. Kiyah had learned early on not to judge people too bad, and she knew that Mercedes needed a friend now more than ever so she had to play the role; but she would be damned if she allowed her to stay with a piece of shit like Maine forever.

She made her way back to the table and Major was staring at every move she made.

"You're just so damn beautiful, I can't help but to stare. My folks gon' love yo ass."

"Your folks? Did your baby mama meet your folks too?" Kiyah finally addressed the issue.

"I know that's been on the tip of yo tongue all day... but check this out. Listen to me and listen to me real good. I'll always keep it a buck wit you. That girl you saw me wit, Nisha... she's my ex, but she ain't pregnant by me. I ain't been wit her in a year or so and that was my first time seeing her in a hot minute. She popped up to tell me that she was pregnant. She broke my trust in a relationship and that shit was dead, but she helped me a lot throughout the years and I'll always have mad respect for her. She won't be a problem in our relationship. In the business I'm in, there can be a lot of fuckery, but don't let nobody fuck up what we got. Ask me anything and I'll always be honest," he laid everything out.

Kiyah could tell that Major was being sincere and that drew her to him that much more.

"Who said we in a relationship?"

"I did... you gon' challenge me?" he quizzed.

Before Kiyah could answer, the waitress appeared and sat their food down in front of them. Kiyah didn't waste any time picking up her Philly steak and taking a bite. She looked over at Major and his eyes were closed.

"Damn, I didn't even say grace and look at you," she mumbled after he opened his eyes.

"It ain't too late... my OG wouldn't never let us eat without saying grace so that stuck wit me," he laughed.

"Tell me about your family. They live here?"

Major began talking about his life and Kiyah listened attentively. She could tell that he was a standup guy. He was honest about what he does, but Kiyah was impressed that he also had legit businesses and had a solid retirement plan. Before it was time for her to share her story, his phone rang and she could tell by the look on his face that it was important.

"Sorry baby... I gotta answer this," Major told her while swiping the bar across his iPhone to answer.

"Fuck... I'm on my way," he ended the call just that fast.

"Some shit just happened... put your number in my phone and I'ma call you later. We'll go on a real date and finish this," he slid her his phone.

Kiyah didn't waste any time putting her number in his phone. She couldn't lie and say that she wasn't disappointed because she was really enjoying him.

"I promise I'ma make this up to you," he kissed her forehead and left Kiyah with soaked panties.

8

Major couldn't believe he had to dip out on Kiyah so suddenly, but one thing about him, he was about his business no matter what. God must have been on his side earlier and sent him to the café. He was only headed in for a second but when he looked near the back and spotted her, his plans instantly changed. Major peeped ol' buddy still lurking in the shadows damn near the whole time, but he was unbothered because he knew his ass was a lame. Speeding down 285, Major couldn't believe the shit one of the workers had just told him. What a way to fuck up his Saturday morning. After exiting the interstate and speeding down a few side streets, Major pulled up to one of his spots and saw nothing but flames. He parked on the side of the road and then got out, making his way towards where the crowd was.

"Yo what the fuck happened out here?" he fumed.

Sirens could be heard in the distance so knew Major knew cops and a fire truck was near.

"Is it clean in there?" he asked another question.

"Yeah it's clean boss... we was just pulling up and a black Impala rolled by and shot some shit in there and then BOOM!" Pierre explained.

"Where June at wit the shit?"

"He left right when I called you. We knew that shit had to get outta here."

"Yeah good looking out... now we gotta find out what fuck niggaz round here playing games and shit," Major gritted as he pulled out his phone and sent out a few texts.

He let his tech guy know to disable and secure the surveillance and he also sent a text to the cop he had on his payroll. Everyone knew anything could happen at any given time in the streets, and that was one of the reasons Major knew he couldn't do that shit forever. Two firetrucks and two cop cars pulled up simultaneously, and Major prepped Pierre one more time to make sure his story was solid. When the cops walked up with their notepads, Pierre put on a show. Major wanted to call Tyler Perry up and get the nigga an acting job because he was on his shit. One thing about all of their spots, they had shit in them like someone actually lived there. They were insured and every damn thang and the location they were currently at was in Pierre's name, which was why he led the show. Although Major made sure everyone ate good, there were a select few people that had been down with him since the very beginning, so of course they got more than the others knew.

Almost two hours later, Major left the city and headed out to Duluth where he rested is head. Absolutely no one knew about his home there, and he wanted to keep it that way for the time being. During his drive, Major's phone rang and he answered the FaceTime call right away when he saw who it was.

"What's up beautiful?" he smiled as he placed his iPhone in the port to keep from holding it while driving.

"You always have so much charm? How's my baby doing today? You look a little stressed."

It was crazy how his mom knew him like she knew the back of her hand.

"You swear you know somebody," Major chuckled.

"Boy, I carried your ass for nine months and three days... went through eight hours and fifteen minutes of labor and..."

"I know I know... I'm good tho ma."

"Hmph... if you say so? Any new prospects? Are you not over that Kinisha character yet?"

"I don't know why you don't like Nisha, but no worries on that. She's about to have a baby soon."

"Not by you I hope!" his mom raised her voice.

"Nah... but you'll be happy to know I do have a prospect. Matter fact, I'ma take her out tonight."

"Oooh, you really like her. You should see how you smiling and shit. She better not be a lil gold digger."

"Didn't you raise me right?" Major asked.

"I raised your sister too, but Lord knows she don't know how to pick 'em."

That reminded Major that he needed to call Yanna. It had been almost a week since they talked, and if Major remembered correctly, he was supposed to have called her back. He talked to his mom until he pulled into his garage and promised that he would be there to visit soon. With the way that she was fussing, you would have thought that he didn't just leave California the month before.

"Your dad will be in Georgia soon... just giving you a heads up," Carolyn told him and quickly hung up.

Major made a mental note to call her back later to get the details. Even though his dad was retired, he still stayed in the know, and if he had planned a trip without telling Major, he could only assume that something was going on. Once Major was inside, he went straight to his bar and poured himself a stiff drink. The day started out great then went downhill, but Major was going to make it his business to end it on a good note. Major called Duke and chopped it up with him and then a couple of other investors to make sure that shit was on task. When he was satisfied with everything, it was damn near four o'clock. Major had been mentally preparing what he wanted to do later while handling business and decided that he would take Kiyah out to Lake Lanier for a night cruise and dinner. He sent a text to set everything up and then sent her a text.

Major: Send me your address and be ready by 6

Kiyah: Send me the address to where you want me to meet you and I'll be there by 7

Major couldn't do shit but laugh at her feisty ass. He wasn't even mad; he had to respect her independence.

Major: You making this harder than it has to be Miss Kiyah

Kiyah: That's what I do (winking emoji)

He forwarded her the address and then got up to start getting ready himself. As soon as Major turned on the water in the shower, his phone chimed.

Kiyah: You ain't tryna drown me are you?

Major: Only wit love baby

Major chuckled at her antics and knew that Miss Kiyah was about to take him on a ride, but he was ready for it.

9

Ever since Raina had posted pictures of her hair and tagged her, Mercedes had been getting all types of calls for appointments. She was fully booked for the next two weeks and as if God was on her side, Maine had been working from morning til night. He wasn't happy about having to actually put in work that demanded all of his time, but Mercedes damn sure was. She loved the freedom that his absence provided her and most times, he was so tired that he had no time to pick any fights with her. Maine hadn't gone into much detail about the reason for him working so much, but he'd only told her that there were issues at one of the houses so he had to oversee things for a while. In her opinion, it was one of the best things that could have happened because it was indirectly helping their relationship. Not in a huge way but enough that she wasn't feeling so smothered and she wasn't sporting any bruises either, which was a blessing.

That morning, he'd left before her and Baby J had even woken up, and since she was scheduled to do somebody's hair, Kiyah had come over to get the baby for her. She loved spending time with her Godson and had made plans for them to go to Chucky Cheeses. Since the girl stayed next door to her, Mercedes figured that she would complete her side part bob and still have time to meet up with them. She couldn't lie, she felt slightly funny going right next door to do some hair, especially when she hadn't even realized that they had new neighbors. It was a huge possibility that they had heard her and Maine on more than one occasion fighting, so she planned to keep it to herself that she lived so close.

Mercedes gathered her bag with her supplies and checked herself out in the floor length mirror that rested next to the front door. She'd decided to wear a pair of light blue distressed jeans with a white sweatshirt that had Balenciaga stamped all over it in bold black letters and some black checkered, high top Vans. Her natural hair was in a simple up/down style and she rocked a pair of silver hoops. Mercedes always looked runway ready without even trying, but with Maine not there to dictate her style, she decided to put a little bit more effort into her look for the day. She snapped a quick picture for Instagram with the caption "natural glow" and was out the door.

Trying to keep up appearances, she drove the short distance and parked in the circular driveway right behind a black on black G-wagon. Before she could even get out of the car, the girl, Dreka, was standing in the doorway with a wide grin as a nigga loomed behind her with an angry scowl plastered on his face. In an effort to not read too much into the situation, she still got out with her bag and a smile of her own, which quickly disappeared when she got to the steps and realized that it was the same nigga from Five Guys. She was ready to back pedal right up outta there, but Dreka grabbed her by the hand and pulled her inside.

"Get back Duke, you already got her scared to come in!" Dreka huffed with an eye roll before turning back to Mercedes. "It's okay girl, he's just over paranoid. Thanks so much for coming over, you a whole beast out here." She continued to talk, not noticing the stare down that was happening right in front of her.

Mercedes certainly hadn't thought she'd ever run across the asshole who'd made her move her car that day, especially at a client's house. Not sure if he remembered her or not, she took the opportunity to admire him, even though she was still quite pissed about the whole thing. Her body lit up as he did the same, letting his eyes roam her from top to bottom before licking his already juicy lips.

"Anyway, I'm glad I came across you! We just moved here and I didn't know any good stylists, so you're a straight lifesaver!" She gushed. "Now this is my big brother Duke, or Dookie, as I like to call him and Duke, this is Mercedes," she introduced the two excitedly. Mercedes wasn't sure why, but she felt a sense of relief upon hearing that Dreka wasn't his girlfriend, wife, or baby mama. She suddenly became hyper aware of the huge rock on her finger and wished that she'd taken it off but just as quickly chastised herself. *Duke* was a rude asshole and not only that, she was already in a relationship with a whole son and a wedding on the way. She didn't need to add to her already complicated life, and she could tell that messing around with him would be a straight up disaster.

Instead of bringing up that they'd already sort of met or apologizing, Duke mumbled a weak ass "what's up" and brushed past her and out of the door. Despite having already surmised that he was mean as hell, Mercedes still found herself shocked as she watched him swagger to the G-wagon and pull off.

"Sorry about that, he's not usually *that* rude." His sister apologized, looking after him also with her face scrunched in confusion.

"Sure he ain't." Mercedes thought she said under her breath but Dreka looked her way and chuckled, letting her know that she'd heard her.

"Well, come on, I got us all set up in the dining room." Dreka closed the huge wooden door and led her through the house. "Don't mind all these boxes and shit. I told Duke to hire somebody to set everything up cause I sure as hell ain't bouta do it." She waved around the cluttered living room as she walked. Honestly, the last thing that Mercedes was thinking about was the stacks of boxes and furniture. Her mind was still on the man that had just left, wondering how somebody so handsome could be such a dick.

"Oh I understand, shit I hate having to unpack too." Mercedes let her know and sat her bag down on one of the many chairs that surrounded the long dining room table where Dreka stopped. She had her bundles, needle, thread, a comb, and edge control already set out, which Mercedes was impressed with. Dreka let her know that she'd already washed her hair, so Mercedes was able to start on her braids as soon as she sat down. The two made light conversation where she found out that Dreka was eighteen and had recently been allowed to graduate early since she made such good grades. Her and Duke came from Chicago to there because he'd gotten a better paying job; just from meeting him, Mercedes knew that meant he was in the streets. She couldn't blame Dreka for wanting to protect her brother because she had and still would do the same for Maine. She could tell that the two were close and that often Duke was over protective, and while Dreka complained about how annoying it was, it wasn't stopping her from going off to college like he preferred. Mercedes wished she had the option to go to somebody's school, but after graduating high school and giving birth to Baby J, Maine had flat out refused. He claimed that he wanted her there to take care of their son when really it was all about having her close and not allowing her any independence. She could admit that she loved being able to be a stay at home mom, but she also liked to make her own money. That's why she'd sneakily had an online bank account and had her customers pay her through her cash app. If she didn't know anything else, it was to never let your left hand know what the right hand was doing.

When Mercedes was about halfway done with Dreka's hair, they heard Duke entering the house and her heart instantly started beating a little harder. Although she shouldn't have, she was anticipating seeing him again, even if his ignorant ass had something smart to say. His Hermès cologne rounded the corner before he did, and Mercedes' clit throbbed at the sight of him-- the man was pure perfection. Without speaking, he came over, standing so close that she was sure he could hear her breathing pick up as he looked over her work with cold eyes.

"Why her head look like a beehive in the middle with hair coming out of it?" He questioned, looking confused as hell. Mercedes tried her hardest not to laugh at the puzzled expression on his face, but she couldn't stop herself. The thing that was so funny was that he was serious.

"She not finished yet duh!" Dreka chimed with a chuckle.

"Shiiit, I hope not! Yo ass look like a Cynthia doll by the head!" That time he too had an amused smirk on his face as he shared a look with Mercedes.

"Forget you punk!" Dreka turned slightly in the chair and popped his arm playfully.

"Man, I was bouta go hop on the game, but now I gotta see how the fuck she gone fix this." Duke said before pulling out one of the chairs at the table and sitting down. Mercedes couldn't believe that he had a light hearted side, considering how they'd first met, but she definitely liked it much better. That didn't stop her from being nervous under his watchful eyes though. She had to catch herself a few times from fucking up as him and Dreka talked because even though he was speaking to his sister, she could feel his intense stare on her.

Mercedes managed to finish the style, and once she did, Dreka hopped up to find a mirror while Mercedes cleaned the small mess she'd made. She had her back turned as she picked up, but the second she felt Duke's presence behind her, she whipped around to face him. He was close enough to damn near kiss her and she had to take a step back so that she wouldn't get the urge to put her lips on his.

"Wh-What are you doing?" She stuttered, looking around nervously like Maine was about to pop out.

"I just wanna apologize about the other day. I ain't usually *that* uh--"

"Mean? Rude? Petty?" Mercedes raised a brow, causing him to titter as he rubbed his chin thoughtfully.

"Uh yeah, that." He flashed a quick smile. "I was having a fucked up day though, some bullshit had happened, but I shouldn't have took it out on you." The sincerity in his voice made her believe him and just that quickly, he was forgiven.

"Well, I accept your apology and ...I'm sorry about whatever messed up your day." She told him, shyly looking away. When her eyes landed on him again, his face was twisted in confusion at what she'd said, but before he could inquire about it, Dreka loudly returned.

"Yasssss biiiiitch! This shit look fire!" Dreka exclaimed as she entered the room, swinging her head from side to side with a huge grin.

"Yeah girl, it looks so good on you too!" Mercedes added, easing herself away from Duke, but she wasn't quick enough. She could see that Dreka had quieted even though she still held that same grin as she looked between Mercedes and her brother.

"Mmhmm..... well thanks so much for the do. I already sent your payment to your cash app and added a lil something extra." She winked. "Do you have a number where I can reach you when it's time for this to come down and you know...so we can hang out? I'm gonna need a tour guide and you're cool as hell."

"Thanks, and of course we can." Mercedes rattled off her number as she was walked to the door where Dreka gave her a quick hug and waved goodbye. Before pulling off, she checked to ensure that her payment had been received. The tip that Dreka had left her was far more than just a little extra, and she started to go and ask if it was a mistake but thought better of it. As happy as Dreka had been, she was sure that she'd meant to send her the amount she saw. Feeling excited and nervous at the prospect of having a new friend and another chance to see Duke, she finally drove out of their driveway to meet Kiyah.

🦂 10 🦂

"Where you bouta go?" Duke looked up from his spot at the table where he was eating a breakfast of Captain Crunch to see Dreka with a purse and jacket. She smacked her lips, which she knew he hated and flipped her hair.

"If you must know Mr. Nosy, I'm going to the mall with Mercedes." He didn't miss the slick ass smirk on her face, knowing that he had been asking her about shorty ever since she'd come over. As hard as he had tried and as busy as he'd been, Mercedes had been on his mind heavily. Not only was she fine as fuck but she was genuine, which was rare. Duke had met plenty of bitches who wanted something from him, so they played the part and tried to act like they gave a damn about him. Though he allowed them to play themselves, he never had any intentions on offering them more than hard dick, so it didn't really matter. With Mercedes though, he wanted to get to know her, find out things about her, and that surprised the fuck out of him.

"Oh word, I'm bouta slide with y'all then." He said, wiping the smirk right off her face as he stood to go and put his bowl in the dishwasher. Like he knew she would, Dreka followed behind him whining.

"Don't be tryna come just so you can run yo lil weak ass game on her! She cool as hell, and I don't want you getting sucked up into your harem!"

"My game ain't weak at all, and I ain't got no *harem*. I just got one or two shorties I fuck with here and there." Duke shrugged and exited the kitchen to go and get dressed while she called after him. Nothing she said really mattered because he was crashing their shit regardless, so she was wasting her breath. He hurriedly replaced the basketball shorts and t-shirt with a black crew neck sweatshirt and some jeans. Deciding on a pair of fresh Air Force Ones, he slipped his feet into them and threw on a Cuban and a Rolex before lightly spraying himself with some Creed. It turned out to be a good thing that he'd gotten a head start on Dreka by showering as soon as he'd woken up. He didn't put it past her to try and leave if he wasn't ready when she was. Taking the stairs two at a time, he had to slow up so he wouldn't seem so damn eager, even though he was. The second that he reached the last step, a horn blasted outside and he grinned as Dreka passed him on her way to the door. He wasn't going to pay her attitude any mind;, she'd get over whatever was bothering her eventually.

Outside, he watched Mercedes' smile falter briefly when she saw him come out behind his sister.

"Aye, we riding in the Maserati." He called out to Dreka, who stopped and turned to him in irritation before stomping off to the garage. He didn't know about them, but he wasn't about to squeeze his tall ass into that little shit she called a car. Mercedes watched Dreka walk off confused before turning her attention back to him. Duke leaned down into the open window and grinned. "Leave yo car here, we gone take mine."

"*We?*" she blinked rapidly.

"Yeah *we*. What, I'm not invited?" he leaned back with a hand on his chest in mock offense.

"No- I mean, yeah." She stuttered, causing him to laugh at how nervous his presence made her.

"Come on, I know what you mean." He decided to let her off the hook by answering for her and then headed over to where Dreka had pulled up in his car. Without speaking, he motioned for her little annoying ass to get in the back, ignoring her grumbling, and waited as Mercedes gathered her things before coming over too. Duke admired the way that her ass looked in the neon green biker shorts that she wore. Her sweet smelling perfume quickly filled the car as soon as she closed the door behind her.

"Hey girl! Sorry about the tag along." Dreka frowned, leaning into the front seat and rolling her eyes as they pulled off.

"Oh... umm... it's cool." Mercedes shrugged like Duke hadn't just had her damn near speechless back at her car. She could feel his eyes on her, but instead of acknowledging him, she continued to talk back and forth with Dreka.

"Where lil dude at?" he asked, interrupting whatever it was his sister was about to say.

"Uhhh, he's with my bestie Kiyah. She likes to take him sometimes so that I can get a break."

"Does his Pops ever get him?" he was curious to know.

"Sometimes." She dragged, unable to meet his intense gaze. Duke wanted to inquire further about her relationship with her baby daddy, but they had already pulled up to the mall and she hurried to get out before he could. He couldn't deny feeling a small amount of jealousy at the thought of her still fucking around with him. Unable to ask directly, he followed the two girls into the mall, ready to blow a bag.

Hours later, he sat inside of Blue Flame with Major as a bad ass, thick chocolate bitch danced in his lap. Although Mercedes had barely given him any play, he could see it in her eyes that she wanted him; he just needed to figure out what was holding her fine ass back. His mind was so stuck on thoughts of Mercedes that he didn't notice Raina until she was right next to him. She snatched the stripper named Coco off his lap, causing her to screech loudly.

"Get yo thirsty ass outta here bitch!" she growled, tossing her to the side roughly.

"Damn Storm, you ain't have to do all that!" the bitch that had been dancing for Major ran over and helped her friend up.

"Tell her to keep her stank ass off my man then!" Raina didn't pay them anymore attention as she focused on Duke and sat down in the same spot that Coco had been occupying. He'd forgotten that she worked there and instantly regretted it.

"I hope yo stupid ass ain't goin' around tellin' these bitches I'm shit to you other than a nut bitch." He grabbed her face and squeezed hard. Tears filled her eyes but he didn't feel bad at all. Raina's pussy was mediocre at best. The most she had going for her was her neck, and that was all he was keeping her around for.

"I'm sorry Duke. I just get jealous when I see you with these other hoes." She pouted and flexed her jaw once he released her. "Why you ain't called me?"

Duke looked at Major in irritation, but that nigga just laughed at his ass and threw his hands up. He blew air out, hoping to relieve some of his frustrations so that he wouldn't slap Raina dead in her shit. It was like she didn't listen to shit he said when he was talking.

"I call you when I want my dick sucked, if I ain't been calling then that means somebody else is. This shit far from exclusive shorty, don't play yo self." The eager look never left her eyes and it amazed him just how pressed some females were over niggas. Completely turned off, he stood up, cutting off anything she was about to say as she fell to the floor. With his mood ruined, he and Major headed out. He was already on his phone preparing to meet another jump off at the hotel.

"Nigga, you cold as shit with these hoes!" Major laughed once they'd made it outside to their cars.

"Mannn, she was doin' too much. Besides I got my eye on some-thing else right now, on some serious shit though."

"I feel you. Shit, being a playa gets old. I'm tryna seal the deal with this lil shorty Kiyah too. She been giving me a lil push back but that ain't shit." He cheesed. Duke had heard him mention Kiyah a time or two and wondered briefly if it was the same one that ran with Mercedes, but knew that would be too much of a coincidence.

"Let me find out both our asses tryna bag a main!" Duke tittered.

"Well, shit we already got the money and the empire, all that's missin' is our ride or die's." Major said, making a whole lot of sense to Duke's drunken mind. He nodded in agreement just as a text came through, telling him what room number to go to.

"Facts, but while I'm waitin'..." Duke turned the screen so that Major could see it with a grin. Major laughed and shook his head but decided not to preach. He couldn't say that he wasn't on the same type of time himself. The two slapped hands and said their goodbyes before getting into their vehicles.

❧ 11 ❧

It was a nice Saturday in April and the weather was starting to break. Kiyah was dressed comfortably in a floral print maxi dress she had ordered from Fashion Nova and it was hugging every curve on her body. She picked up her paddle brush and ran it through her hair a few times, threw some lip gloss on, and was good to go. As soon as Kiyah walked outside and got in her car, the phone rang. She smiled when she saw that it was Major.

"Hey you!" Kiyah cooed.

"What's up babe? What you on?" Major quizzed.

"Headed to the mall to meet Mercedes and then we gon' eat somewhere. I gotta find a dress and shoes for graduation next month."

"That special day is right around the corner huh?"

"Yup! I'ma turn a cartwheel across the stage," Kiyah laughed.

"I'll be there to record it."

"Aww... you really planning on coming to my graduation?"

"Shawty don't play me like that... you *mine* and I ain't even hit yet; just imagine when I do though."

Kiyah couldn't help but to laugh at Major, but while she was laughing, her pussy was purring too. They had shared countless hugs, kisses, and other intimate moments, but Major hadn't pressured her for sex.

51

She actually wanted him more than him, but she had been trying her best to keep her composure. It had been so damn long since she had some, Kiyah knew that she wouldn't be able to hold out too much longer. They talked for a few more minutes and then Kiyah's mom beeped in, so she told Major that she would call him back later.

"Heeyyy ma!"

"Hey sweetheart. How are you?"

"I'm good. Heading to the mall to find my outfit for graduation. Are you guys driving or being lazy and flying?"

"Lazy? We would just rather get there quick."

"Mom, South Carolina isn't far... Dad can drive that with his eyes closed," Kiyah laughed.

"Forty-five minutes trumps four hours any day of the week. So do I need to make reservations for after graduation or have you made plans?"

Kiyah briefly thought about Major and wondered if she should tell her mom about him. When she thought about how they always wanted her with a lawyer or doctor or even an engineer, she quickly brushed that thought to the side.

"I'll let you know in a week or so. Where's dad?"

"It's Saturday... you know David is golfing," Karen replied.

"Oh yeeaahhh... what was I thinking?"

"Uh oh... Sis Rosie is calling. Let me call you back baby," Karen said and hung up before Kiyah could reply.

Kiyah knew that her parents weren't going to be expecting to meet a man on her graduation day, but she was bracing herself. She was really feeling Major, so she told herself that it was best to make it happen that day. He had been hinting at getting her something, but honestly, Kiyah would just be happy to have his presence there. It had been forever since she entertained a man, and if she had to admit it to herself, it was going to just feel good to have one there for such an important milestone. Traffic was a bitch and due to an accident, it took Kiyah an extra twenty minutes to make it to Lenox. Once she finally arrived, she spotted Mercedes' car near the front entrance and an empty spot was right next to it. She whipped into it before the car turning on that row could grab it.

After grabbing her phone and debit card, Kiyah got out and headed straight for the back door of Mercedes' car.

"Hey handsome," she unbuckled Baby J from his seat and got him out.

"Hey Tee Tee... daddy was mean to mommy again."

Kiyah whipped her head in Mercedes' direction and her eyes bucked. Kiyah could tell that she was embarrassed and that was the first time Baby J had ever said anything like that to her.

"You gotta get this shit together, Mercedes. Your son is paying attention to everything."

"That's okay baby. He won't be mean anymore. Auntie Kiyah is gonna kick his ass okay."

He shook his head yes and Kiyah couldn't do anything but roll her eyes at Mercedes out of pure frustration.

"I know Kiyah... I know. He's kept his hands to himself recently, but I know it's about to change. I don't wanna talk about him anyway. I got some exciting news to share when we eat and the little one is occupied."

Kiyah shrugged off her negative thoughts about Maine and smiled at the glow that Mercedes had at the mention of exciting news. She had her own excitement to share with her best friend and couldn't wait. An hour and a half later, Kiyah settled on her dress and a pair of Louboutin's since it was a special occasion, and they were in Chipotle about to stuff their faces. Kiyah had been feeling like someone had following them ever since they arrived at the mall, but every time she looked, she didn't see anyone. They placed their orders, Mercedes handed Baby J some headphones, and then jumped right into their girl talk session.

"Giiirrrllll... I met this fiiiine ass nigga. His name is Duke. The first time I met his ass, he was so rude, but when I saw him again, I could tell that he's not even like that. Is it possible for me to be feeling another nigga like that while I'm in love wit Maine?"

"First of all... you don't love Maine, you just feel obligated to stay with him because y'all have a child together... now that I got that outta the way, let's focus on this new man. I want alllll of the juicy details before I tell you about my date."

"Date? Wait, you went on a date? My shit can wait. Who you went on a date wit?"

"You ain't off the hook, but Major took me out to Lake Lanier and we had a candlelight dinner on his Yacht girl. It was sooo romantic... oh my gawwddd! He had a damn live jazz band on there, a personal chef, and even a photographer. Look at these pics we took," Kiyah handed Mercedes her phone.

"Awww, y'all look so cute together. I could tell Major was that nigga at the club that night, but I didn't think he had a romantic side. You got a keeper boo," Mercedes chided.

"It feels like I've known him forever. Is that crazy?" Kiyah queried.

"Ion think it's crazy. I kinda feel like I've known Duke a long time and we've only hung out once."

"Wait... y'all hung out? How did that happen? I need all the details."

Mercedes started telling Kiyah about everything and she felt that eerie feeling once again. When Kiyah turned around, she spotted Chris nearby. He had to have seen her, but he was acting like he didn't.

"Chris?" she called out to him.

"Oh hey Kiyah. I didn't even see you."

"You didn't see me sitting here? How long have you been here?"

"No, I didn't and I just got here. It's good to see you though. They just called my order so I'll see you in class next week."

Chris disappeared and Kiyah felt like something was off with him. Mercedes picked her story back up once he was gone. Kiyah was listening, but she couldn't shake the feeling that Chris had been following her. He had been nothing but nice; she chunked it up to her ass being too cautious and hungry at the same time.

❧ 12 ❧

After Major hung up with Kiyah, he made the turn for incoming flights at Hartsfield Jackson Atlanta International Airport. The airport was already crowded as fuck, and the construction made it ten times worse. Major thought about sending a driver to make the pickup, but he knew that it probably wouldn't have gone over too well. He pulled over in the designated area and saw a punk ass security guard heading his way. Before he made it, the door opened and in hopped his old man.

"What up Pops?"

"Hey son... let's get outta here before I have to end one of these punk ass security guards career," his dad shook his head as he hopped in.

Major thought about the last incident his dad had with security and chuckled as he pulled away from the curb. It was good that his mom had given him a heads up because his dad didn't let him know that he was on the way until he was thirty minutes away from landing. Alonzo was like that; it was nothing for him to pop up and expect people to drop whatever they were doing for him. Known to most as Zo, he had that much respect and people honestly didn't mind returning the favor because he treated everyone around him quite well.

"Say no more. How long you here for?"

"If all goes well, I'll be back on the west coast by Monday. Now let's cut straight to the chase. Any leads on who set the house on fire?"

"Should have something solid within forty-eight hours... gotta be this new crew that's calling themselves..."

"The Get Low Crew..." they said in unison and Major looked over at his dad.

"I knew it... so this must be personal for you to fly in?"

"You know it... those lil niggaz got a dumb name just like their folks did. I got a phone call about a month ago about Phillip's boys wanting to destroy you because of what I did to him. Been monitoring them ever since and tomorrow, they'll all be history. Setup a meeting with your crew so I can do a walk through."

"You don't trust me to keep my shit solid. If Unc trusted me, why can't you?" Major wanted to know.

"Major, your uncle trusted you on the strength of me. I know you think..."

"You never really retired. It all makes sense. Last time I asked, you brushed it off, but I see it clear as day now. I been knowing, but why the lies?"

"Your mother has a way of getting information out of you, son... we know this, and I really am retired to the streets, but it never ends. Me being behind the scenes protects you in more ways than one."

Major pondered on what his dad had just said. He wasn't mad, because deep down, he already knew the truth; however, he wished that his dad wasn't so damn secretive. Right then and there, Major knew that Zo was still the connect whose name that no one knew. He picked up his phone and sent a quick text to Duke, letting him know to round the team up. Major made his way to his condo that was located in Hiram so that his dad could change out of his traveling clothes and have a drink before meeting up with the team. He needed to handle a little business also. Almost an hour later, they arrived and Major went straight to the bar and poured a double shot of Crown Black since the bottle near the front was almost gone.

Zo could be heard on the phone and Major knew that he was talking to his mom. He took that time to go into his office and hop on the computer. What he had in mind for Kiyah's graduation gift, most would think that it was over the top, but nothing was over the top for Major Elliot. They hadn't known each other that long, but Major knew that he wanted her in his life... *forever*.

Later that evening, Major and Zo pulled up to the designate meeting area. Major surveyed his surroundings by instinct before and after he got out. The duo made their way inside and upon entrance, everyone greeted them and began dispersing from their cliques. It had been a long time since Zo made an appearance with Major, so confusion was evident on the faces of the new members on the team. All they had to do was take a close look and they would notice the striking resemblance of the two. If you didn't know any better, they could pass for brothers because Zo worked out just as much as Major.

Major got the meeting started and gathered updates first. Afterwards, he talked about the expansion plan that him and Duke had been working on. Maine was sitting in the back and each time Major mentioned Duke's name, he had a sour look on his face. Major took a deep breath before continuing, but he was a little pissed off because he thought Maine had his jealousy under control. He wrapped the meeting up a little while later with the intent on talking to Maine, but one of the other guys stopped him and Maine had disappeared when he was done. Major, Zo, and Duke talked privately after everyone left. It had been a couple of years since Zo had seen Duke, but Zo and his late dad were friends, so Duke had always been treated like he was in the family because he was. Blood couldn't make them any closer.

Once Major and Zo got in his truck to leave, Major already knew what his dad was going to say before he even said it, so he beat him to the punch.

"I got my eyes on him Pops... I'm on it!"

13

Maine irritably finished bagging the large pile of drugs in front of him and glanced at the time. It was already going on midnight and he was ready to go home. Duke's bitch ass had been making him actually work the houses and that meant that he was sitting in a bando from sun up to sun down. As much money he had made Major, he would've never thought that he would let some shit like that go down, but it was clear that Major was siding with Duke. Maine already felt some type of way about the fact that he'd come in dropping orders and demanding shit, but now he was forcing him to work beside their regular ass nickel and dime hustlers. He felt that he was way too deep in the game to be bagging up drugs and shit. He'd put in the work that had afforded him the big house, the fancy cars, and the bad bitch on his arm. Now he had been reduced to working directly with niggas that were under him.

Just the thought had him ready to throw the table across the room, but Maine knew better than to act a damn fool like he wanted. As tough as he pretended to be, the only one who was afraid of him was Mercedes, and he dreaded the day that she realized how much of a fraud he was. The thought of what she could have been doing had him standing with his phone in hand, ready to call and make sure that she was in the house like he'd told her to be. The hours he was working made it impossible for him to keep track of what she was doing every minute of the day like he had before. Not knowing was killing him and he was regretting not installing cameras in his house so that he could keep tabs on her.

"Aye, we ain't finished yet. Duke bringing more work through." Some little young nigga named Dread warned from across the table. Maine resisted the urge to roll his eyes as he looked down at him, instead, he sucked his teeth which was just as feminine.

"Yo lil thirsty ass. I'm bouta make a call, ain't nobody leavin'." He spat frustrated that he even had to answer to anybody, let alone a nigga young enough to still be in high school. Maine didn't wait around for him to reply; although he knew it was some smart shit that came out of his mouth. Niggas around there were acting like Duke was their damn daddies and shit like they were scared he'd pull off his belt.

Instead of dwelling on how soft they all were, Maine hurried into the bathroom and pressed send under Mercedes' contact, only to hear it ring once and go right to voicemail. With his face frowned up, he called ten more times and got the same results. He decided not to leave a message, although he was burning up inside. There was no reason for her to have her phone off when he was out of the house. His mind started wandering if she was even at home; he'd hate to have to kill that silly bitch if she tried to play him like she'd done on Kiyah's birthday. Now he was mad for a whole nother reason and he stomped out of the bathroom ready to say *fuck it* and just leave so he could check on his bitch, but the sight of Duke standing at the table talking to Dread slowed him down. They both looked up as he entered the living room that had been converted into a work station, like they'd been talking about him. He didn't miss the stupid ass smirk that covered Duke's face either.

"I see I'm right on time." He said, motioning towards the table at all of the dope they'd finished bagging up. Maine wished that he could knock the smug ass look off his face without dealing with retaliation, but everyone in the large room had already proven their loyalty to Duke, so he knew he wouldn't even make it outside if he did. Instead of doing what he really wanted to do, he attempted to swallow his pride and made his way over.

"Yeah we finished that shit in no time. But it's already late and I been staying til damn near two every night, so would it be cool if I cut out early?" He questioned in the nicest way possible. Duke's brows drew together before he turned to Dread and they both laughed. Maine looked between the two, not really knowing what the fuck was so funny but didn't ask.

"If you can finish this early then you can fuckin' leave, but not a second before." Duke sneered suddenly, all humor gone as he dropped the bag that was strapped across his chest onto the table, letting the contents spill out. Duke stood with his arms folded, staring at him like he dared Maine to object. Sighing, Maine nodded, prompting Duke to drop his stance and turning to slap hands with Dread. "Ayite, I'ma leave y'all to it then."

Maine watched defeated as Duke said bye to everybody before heading to the door. After that, you would think that he wouldn't want to keep bothering him, but he just had to know how much longer the shit was going to continue. Without a word, he followed Duke out the door and caught him right before he was rounding the front of his G-wagon.

"Ayo Duke!" He called, hoping that he would stop his stride; but that nigga kept walking, only pausing just as he opened the door, indicating that he wasn't going to give him much time. Without saying shit, he looked back at Maine coming down the stairs with a mixture of irritation and amusement evident on his face.

"Make it quick."

"I... uh, I just wanna know how much longer you gone have me workin' in here doin' this menial shit? Ain't I worked that shit off yet?" Maine was damn near whining and even though the nigga had just tried to chump him inside, he wasn't expecting the cold ass look Duke suddenly gave him.

"You gone work here til I say you done nigga! I don't like people wasting my time, it's like saying *fuck you* to me. And since time is some shit I can't get back, you gone be doin' this *menial shit* until I feel like my time has been compensated." He gritted and without waiting for a reply, although there was none, Duke slid inside his car and pulled off.

"Bitch ass nigga!" Maine shouted angrily as he watched the lights disappear into the darkness. He should have known that Duke was going to try him, but he'd figured if they were alone, it would be no reason for him to throw his weight around. Obviously, he'd been wrong. He was still sitting outside fuming as he smoked the small piece of blunt he'd had in his pocket. Duke had managed to make him even more upset than he already was and he needed to relieve some pressure somehow. Since Mercedes' face wasn't readily available, he definitely planned on waking her up to an ass whooping no matter how tired he was.

"That nigga ain't untouchable you know." A voice said from behind him. Maine turned around surprised to see the outline of someone sitting on the porch's banister. The nigga had obviously been out there the entire time. Maine eyed the unknown person suspiciously until he stepped out and into the light that was flooding the porch from the living room. He instantly recognized him as a worker named Chris, but he still didn't say anything to acknowledge him. "I'm just sayin', you ain't gotta keep letting him come at you reckless." Chris added, flicking his cigarette over the side of the porch.

"Man fuck that nigga!" Maine huffed, waving in the direction that Duke had drove off into. He couldn't help but be embarrassed that somebody else had witnessed their conversation, but he didn't want to seem like a bitch.

"Shit I feel you man. That nigga came through tryna boss up on everybody like he *been* here. I can't stand his ass and the way these lil muhfuckas jump when he talk. It's actually good to see that I ain't the only one though." Maine gave him a questioning glance as he stepped closer. He too felt like everybody had bowed at that nigga's feet the minute he was introduced to them. The only other person who had shared in his contempt was his right hand Petey, but they were still outnumbered, considering that no one else had openly spoken out until now. That didn't stop him from wondering if the nigga Chris was setting him up though. He'd only known him for the month or so that he'd been working the house, and this was the first time that he'd ever spoken ill about Duke. Noticing his hesitancy, Chris leaned in as if someone else might hear, even though they were alone.

"Look, I know you probably skeptical and shit, I would be too. But at the end of the day, we got a common enemy and instead of just talking shit bout the nigga, let's do something to eliminate the problem. It's power in numbers."

Maine pondered over what he'd just said, wondering if it would be in his best interest to go after Duke. It was true that he hadn't done anything besides gripe about the nigga, but at the time, that was really all that he could do. With another man on board, it made him feel as if there may be more niggas willing to get rid of his ass, but they would have to be smart about it because going up against Duke would mean going up against Major too. Considering that he'd been the one to even bring Duke around to step on their toes anyway, Maine really didn't feel no type of way about crossing his friend. Not when Major had technically crossed him first by overlooking him. For the first time that day, Maine let a smile cross his face at the thought of possibly taking Duke down.

"What you have in mind?"

14

Duke ignored another call from Raina and went back to his messaging screen so that he could text Mercedes a "good morning beautiful." He'd put it right in his phone the day that she gave it to Dreka and had been calling and texting her on the regular. Although at first, she seemed apprehensive when she found out it was him, she'd since loosened up and he'd learned a lot about her. Their conversations always flowed effortlessly and he had to admit that he really fucked with her. She was fine as hell and had a good head on her shoulders, despite having a hating ass baby daddy that didn't want her to better herself. That was just one of the many things that she had opened up to him about since they'd been talking. He wasn't usually the type to step on a nigga's toes, but from everything that she'd told him about the nigga led him to believe that ol' dude was a bitch. Besides being controlling and not allowing her to go to work or school, the nigga damn near held her hostage in the house most times. She'd only recently gotten any freedom from that nigga and she barely had that. Duke felt like she was one step away from being a battered woman, considering all the shit she was going through with him already, but leaving would have to be her choice. Duke knew that if he forced her, then there was a chance that Mercedes would go back and he wasn't even trying to put himself through that drama.

Mercedes texted back right away with a "gm" and the heart emoji eyes, causing Duke to smirk at how she was trying to play him. If he knew her address, he would've gone over there and spanked her fine ass, but he would get that shortly. Duke had Major's tech man looking into shorty and he expected some type of information that day. His phone rang again in his hand, bringing him out of his thoughts. He was going to ignore it, thinking it was Raina's ass again. He was glad to see though that it was Major and he answered right away.

"What's up bro? How yo lil date night go?" He asked as soon as the call connected.

"Shiiit, it woulda been great, but my ass had to fly out and see bout Yanna's ass. She got into a car accident last night." He sighed and Duke jumped out of bed ready to catch a flight himself.

"Nigga, what happened?! How she doin'? Is she straight? Is you straight?" Duke shot off question after question as he slipped into a pair of joggers and a t-shirt.

"Mann, it was some fucking drunk driver, but thankfully, she's cool besides a few bumps and bruises. We all good out this way, plus I got Kiyah with me, so I'm a hundred." He assured, causing Duke to stop what he was doing as a slow grin spread across his face.

"Aw damn! You done introduced shorty to the fam already and you ain't even hit yet!"

"Who the fuck said I ain't hit?"

"My ass just missing everything." Duke grumbled, sitting back down on the edge of his bed.

"This shit just happened last night bro, but damn it was worth the wait. Shorty's ass bet not *ever* try and leave me. I'll probably fuck around and kill a nigga." He joked, although he was dead ass serious.

"This nigga sprung!" Duke threw his hands up in mock exasperation, but he was really happy for his boy and couldn't wait to meet the woman who'd made his homey throw in his player's card.

"Man, I can't even lie... I'm gone off Kiyah's fine ass."

Duke could hear it all in his voice how happy he was and was glad that everything had turned out okay. He could rest a little bit easier knowing that his boy was straight.

"We bouta head back up to the hospital though, but I probably won't be back for another day at least, hold that shit down for me."

"You already know." Duke said and the two friends hung up. As soon as he was off the phone, he slid his feet into his black Nike slides and went in search of some type of breakfast. Since Dreka didn't have no intentions on doing anything domestic and he really didn't have time, he'd broken down and finally hired a maid and some movers to help unpack them. He'd made sure to thoroughly threaten them, so they knew better than to try and steal anything out of his shit. So far, they'd done a good job and was almost finished setting up the downstairs area since he wouldn't allow them upstairs. Even the little maid Isabella's old ass wasn't allowed up there. It wasn't that he kept anything in the house really, but Duke just didn't feel comfortable with strangers moving around his shit.

He reached the first floor and immediately noticed that Isabella had already arrived and was setting up everything her little old fragile body could handle. She'd organized the bookshelf and some of their pictures already and had even done some vacuuming, which was evident from the fruity ass smell emanating from the living room. With a nod of appreciation at how everything was coming together, Duke continued on to the kitchen, making himself a bowl of Fruit Loops and took a seat at the island.

After finishing his cereal without running into his sister or Isabella, he grabbed the keys to his Maserati and headed out to do the pickups. The sun shined brightly and a little breeze was present but not enough to make him regret coming out without a jacket on. He slid behind the wheel and started down the street when he saw a female walking down the driveway of the house next door. Duke had to do a double take when he realized that it was Mercedes and she was carrying her son. She was walking toward the street with nothing on but a thin ass short silk night gown and nothing even on her feet. Her face was red and he could tell that she was crying as she repeatedly wiped her face.

Slamming on the breaks and reversing until he was right back in front of Mercedes, Duke immediately got out, startling her.

"Give him here and get in." He ordered, not leaving room for argument as he took the sleepy baby from her arms. Without another word, he carried Baby J to the car, not even checking to see if Mercedes was behind him. Duke was heated as fuck; the fact that Mercedes lived next door meant that *she* was the one getting her ass beat over there. He hadn't expected her to disclose certain things about her personal life, but at the same time, he was mad that she hadn't told him-- a complete contradiction. Lifting the front seat, he made sure to buckle her son in, even though they were only going next door. Duke didn't play around about seat belts no matter the distance, especially where a baby was concerned.

After making sure that little man was straight in the back seat, Duke got in himself, unable to look Mercedes' way as he reversed to his driveway and pulled back inside. She cried silently beside him, but he still didn't say anything as he sat with his eyes straight ahead, trying to calm down and also trying to figure out why he was so damn mad.

"Duke.... It's not what you think." Mercedes sobbed as she exploded into another fit of tears and he finally drew his eyes her way.

"Oh, so it's *not* like yo *abusive ass nigga* didn't put you and yo son out before you even had time to get dressed?" He raised a brow at her as if to dare her to lie again.

"I-I--"

"Why you ain't tell me that nigga was putting his hands on you?" He fumed, cutting her off. She looked at him wide eyed and suddenly angry about him being mad that she was a victim of domestic violence. It felt like he was judging her, without knowing the full story.

"For what?" She finally snapped, glaring at him.

"What?"

"What should I have told you for? Huh? What you was gone *save* me? Take care of me and my son in exchange for some pussy? Why do you even care any fuckin' way?! Nobody else do!" Her raising her voice startled her son, who immediately started to cry too, probably thinking that they were about to start fighting.

"Aye, I'm tryna help yo simple ass... I don't gotta do that just for some pussy. Now why I give a fuck? I really don't know, but I do. *That* should count for something, so bring yo ass in here so you can get some clothes on and something to eat." Duke demanded, getting out of the car and taking her son with him. Either Mercedes was going to bring her silly ass in or she was gone sit out there in his car. Whichever she chose, at least she wouldn't be walking around outside like nobody loved her ass. As far as he was concerned, he had done his good deed and extended an olive branch. It would be up to her whether she accepted it or not.

15

"Kiyah... you wanna umm... would you like to go out tonight? Like to the movies or something?" Chris asked her after class. Ever since Major made Chris leave their study date, Kiyah had only conversed with him between classes. He told her that his dad had him pulling extra hours, but Kiyah didn't mind because Major had been taking up all of her spare time. The semester was almost over and she was pretty confident with everything. Chris asking her on a date date did surprise her though.

"Umm... I actually have plans Chris. And I thought..."

"Never mind. Forget I asked. I'll see ya around," Chris said and disappeared before Kiyah could respond.

She wasn't trying to hurt his feelings, but Kiyah did have plans for the night after she got off work. Her job on campus ended the week before, but she had to do a four hour shift at Footlocker. She was scheduled to start a paid internship the next month out in Duluth for a fortune five hundred company, and Kiyah was excited about it. Most of her paychecks normally went to shoes, but she had been buying business attire from New York & Company and Express recently. After changing clothes, Kiyah left campus dressed in her black and white striped shirt, shorts, and a pair of Jay's, ready for work.

An accident delayed traffic, but Kiyah was still able to make it to work and clock in right on time. The store wasn't too packed since it was early, but Kiyah knew the crowd would be coming through soon. She didn't mind being busy because it helped the time to fly by. The only days she hated working were when Jordan's were released. Kiyah avoided those days at all costs because niggaz just didn't know how to act.

"Welcome to Footlocker... can I help you with anything in particular?" Kiyah asked a lady who walked in with a little boy who appeared to be two or three years old. The little boy reminded her of Baby J so much.

"Yes... we're looking for a couple pair of shoes for lil man here," the girl smiled.

"He's such a cutie... follow me," Kiyah complimented and then led them to the area where toddler sizes were located.

She suggested a few pair and sized the little fella and disappeared to the back to retrieve the correct sizes. When she made it back, the lady had another pair in her hands. It was actually the same pair that Kiyah had copped for Baby J the week before. They exchanged shoes and when Kiyah came back, she stopped at the door and snapped a picture of the little boy so that she could show Mercedes the resemblance between the two. They said everyone had a twin somewhere, and she had found Baby J's twin on a random day at work. After settling on three pair of shoes, Kiyah was done with them and on to the next.

Five o'clock rolled around pretty fast and Kiyah was out the door. She headed straight to Publix to gather items for the night. Kiyah felt her phone vibrate and pulled it out, smiling at the text from Major. After replying, she made her way inside the grocery store and picked up everything she needed and was out within twenty minutes. Kiyah made her way home and received a phone call from an unknown number. Since she had been putting her resume out there, she answered when she normally would've allowed an unsaved number to go to voicemail.

"Hello."

"Hi, may I speak with Kiyah Davis?"

"This is she."

"Hi Kiyah. I'm calling from JLL. We have some great news for you..."

Kiyah smiled from ear to ear as she listened to the lady not only offer her an intern but a full time position. She couldn't believe her ears when she heard the pay, but the lady informed her it was because she did a volunteer intern with the company while she was obtaining her Bachelor's. Everything seemed too good to be true, but Kiyah knew that her hard work was paying off and she couldn't be prouder. After agreeing to meet with the company in a week, Kiyah hung up and made a detour and headed towards the liquor store. The night was about to turn into a double celebration.

Once Kiyah made it home, she unloaded the groceries and sat everything on the island. She poured herself a glass of D'usse and cranberry juice and connected her phone to the Bose speaker to get in her zone. It had been forever since she cooked for a man. After seasoning the steaks, Kiyah placed them in a container so that they could soak in Worcestershire Sauce. She put the potatoes in the oven and started on the asparagus. Once that was done, Kiyah went to her bathroom and turned the shower on. Major was supposed to be there at eight o'clock and he was very prompt when it came to time, so Kiyah had an hour a half to spare. She planned on cooking the steaks as soon as he arrived and the potatoes would be done by then too, so everything was on schedule.

After letting the hot water relax her, Kiyah washed her body with some exfoliating Dove and a couple of times before rinsing off. Kiyah dried off and lotioned up with some body butter. She got dressed in a black negligee and pulled her graduation shoes from the box and slipped them on, telling herself that she might as well break them in. At five minutes to eight, her phone rang and it was Major letting her know that he was outside. Kiyah unlocked the door right as Major knocked and then opened it.

"Dammnnn... I think I wanna skip dinner and get straight to dessert," Major asserted and pulled Kiyah in for a hug.

Kiyah couldn't miss the big ass bulge that poked through his jeans.

Her pussy began throbbing and for a minute, she wanted to take Major up on his offer.

"We got time for that," she kissed him repeatedly before ending the kiss and headed towards the kitchen. Major smacked her on the ass and made it jiggle, triggering her to stop and twerk for him. If a slow song wouldn't have been playing in the background, she definitely would have.

Thirty minutes later, Kiyah was fixing their plates while Major poured their drinks. He ended up helping her with the steaks, even though she had it, but it felt good to cook together. Major said grace and then they dug in.

"Smart, beautiful, and can cook... I can't wait to wife you up,' Major proclaimed.

"Oh, you wanna *wife* me up huh?" she flirted.

"Hell yeah... in due time."

Kiyah ate some more of her food and then told Major about her job offer. She would be an occupancy planner and a business consultant. He expressed how proud he was of her and she knew that he was sincere. After they finished eating, Major offered to do the dishes, shocking the hell out of Kiyah.

"You're just *too* good to be true... have you let all ya lil hoes go? Because I know you ain't all the way single."

"I had a few jump offs, but ever since I laid eyes on you, you been the *only* one I wanted," he lifted her chin and expressed, glazing directly into her soul.

Since Kiyah had on her heels, she was able to kiss his lips with ease. One thing led to another and before she knew it, Major had her up on the counter with her legs wide opened, ripping the thin piece of clothing from her delicate body that had been torturing him all night since she opened her door. Finding his destination, he inserted two fingers into her slippery wet center, producing salacious moans to escape her lips. As Major made a trail of fiery kisses on every part of her body that was exposed, sending titillating urges to her nether region, his phone rung, stopping him briefly, but he ignored it. Major's phone rang again and Kiyah knew that he was about to take the call.

"Sorry babe," he apologized, pecked her lips, and then answered it.

"What happened?... Shit!... I'm on my way!" he ended the call and gave her a sympathetic look, and Kiyah knew her disappointment was showing on her face.

🐾 16 🐾

"I'm sorry baby... that was my OG. Something is wrong so I gotta go."

"I understand," Kiyah mumbled.

Major turned to leave and then stopped. He thought about how something always came up when he was spending time with Kiyah, and he didn't want that to become their routine

"Go throw a jogger or something and let's dip. I'll buy you whatever else you need," he told her as he sent out a few texts.

Kiyah must have sensed his urgency, because she didn't question anything and was back within two minutes ready to roll, not having any idea where they were even going. To Major, that meant she trusted him and that gesture meant a lot to him. Kiyah locked up her apartment and they left out. Major was trying to remain calm on the outside, but he was worried within. The only thing he heard his mom say was that Yanna was in the hospital. He didn't need to hear anything else. When it came to his family, he would drop any and everything. Thirty minutes later, Major was turning onto the jet strip. It was good that the jet the family rented had been fixed since he had an emergency. When his dad was in town, the jet was down for repairs, which was why he had to call Major with the few minutes in advance that he did.

"Is everything okay?" Kiyah asked him once they were finally on and seated.

"My sister... I don't know what happened, but she in the hospital so I gotta get there."

"Oh we goin' to Cali? Okay then."

"Yep. I didn't plan on you meeting my folks like this, but this means a lot to me. You literally got ready on spot without asking questions."

"This feeling I get when I'm wit you... it's... it's really hard to explain, but I love it," Kiyah admitted.

"I feel the same way shawty."

The pilot let them know that they were clear for take-off and instructed them to fasten their seatbelts. Both Major and Kiyah followed the commands and were off in no time. Major closed his eyes and found himself praying. Kiyah laid her head on his shoulder and in no time, she was fast asleep. Major didn't realize that he had fallen asleep until a little turbulence woke him up and noticed that they were landing. Kiyah stirred a little and then finally woke up. Major sent a text to his mom and told her to drop their location. The driver was there ready and waiting. As soon as they got off, Major led Kiyah to the black Suburban and they both hopped in the back seat.

"Get us to Kaiser," Major instructed as he closed the door.

"Everything is gonna be okay," Kiyah squeezed his leg.

He leaned over and kissed her while silently praying that she was right. Major hung up on his mom before she could say what was happening because he didn't want to add to his worrying. A part of him did want to know so that he could be prepared, the other part told him to just wait it out. Traffic was thick because it was L.A., but since it was almost midnight, it wasn't the worst. They made it to the hospital and Major called his mom before they arrived at the entrance. She let him know that they were on the Critical Care floor and his heart sank, fearing the worst. As soon as they got off the elevator, his mom was standing there waiting with tears still in her eyes.

"What happened ma? Is Yanna alright?"

"She's in surgery... some drunk driver hit her head on," Carolyn sobbed.

"What they saying though? She gon' be alright?" Major queried.

"You know your sister is a fighter. She will be just fine," his dad appeared and answered.

Major stood there thinking about what his mom said. A damn drunk driver hit his baby sister head on. That brought back so many memories and he knew that his mom was crying for more reasons than one. Her only sister had been killed by a drunk driver while she was crossing the street. The driver ran a red light and hit her along with one other lady who died also. She had pretty much forbidden them from ever drinking and driving, and Major actually listened to her. If he had more than one drink, he would always chill and let it wear off or call a driver.

"Oh my... who do we have here?" his mom finally noticed Kiyah.

"Hello Mrs. Elliot. I'm Kiyah, Major's ummm..."

"Woman... don't try that *friend* shit," he cut her off and lightened the mood, causing everyone to chuckle a little.

"Well I know she's more than a friend if you brought her here. You've never brought anyone here with you... except that..."

"Chill out ma."

"Yeah, don't start Carolyn," Zo added.

"Well Miss Kiyah, you're beautiful and I hope that son of mine is treating you right."

"Thank you so much... you're beautiful yourself, and I actually have no complaints. Major is the best," Kiyah beamed.

"Elliot family," someone called out and Zo led the way to the black woman wearing a white coat.

"Ayanna is out of surgery and she's resting. We were able to stop the internal bleeding and give her some blood. God was on her side because as bad as that bleeding was, she doesn't have any ruptures inside or broken bones. She does have quite a few bruises and sprains so she is heavily sedated, but with the proper rest and exercises, she will be back to herself in no time. Once they get her situated, we will allow you all to visit with her for a little while, but after that, you all will have to come back in the morning," the doctor explained.

"Thank you so much doctor," Carolyn hugged her.

They all thanked her and Major knew what was coming next.

"I'm not leaving my baby here," Carolyn fussed.

"I'm already on it," Zo informed her.

About ten minutes later, they were allowed to go and visit with Yanna for about thirty minutes. She opened her eyes for a few seconds at a time, but the meds were kicking her ass. Major and Kiyah left once the nurse came back, but his parents stayed just like he knew they would. The driver was still waiting and Major had him to take them to his parents' house. He made a list of things for him to pick up bright and early the next morning while they were on the way. Even though he had a few clothes there, he still put some items on the list. They just needed enough to get by until he could take Kiyah shopping. Since Yanna was pretty much okay, he planned to make the trip worthwhile in more ways than one.

It was damn near two o'clock when they made it to the house, which meant it was five o'clock eastern time and Major's body was feeling it. He knew Kiyah had to be exhausted too, but she was hanging in there like a champ. Major saw all of the guards on their posts. To the untrained eye, they would never be seen, but he learned everything at an early age. After the last visit from his dad, everything was crystal clear, and he still didn't know how he had overlooked the shit. They made their way inside after Major unlocked the door and headed straight for his room.

"You want anything to eat or drink?" he asked Kiyah.

"I just want a shower, a comfy bed, and a pillow," she yawned.

"Bet that up," Major led the way to his room.

He grabbed two sets of towels from the hallway closet while on the way. After handing Kiyah a set, he pointed to the bathroom and she wasted no time going inside. Major went and took a piss in the bathroom that was near the living room. When he made it back to his room, he could hear the shower running and a thought popped into his head. He stripped out of his clothes and hoped that Kiyah didn't lock the bathroom door. After twisting the knob, it opened instantly and he made his way to the stainless steel shower. It was almost as if she was waiting on him because she didn't jump or anything.

Major slid inside and wrapped his arms around Kiyah's body. She felled back into him and his penis stood at attention. He began kissing her neck and shoulders and her sexy moans made his throbbing dick harder. Major turned Kiyah around and began sucking on her erect nipples. When she lifted her leg around his body, that was all the invitation he needed. He entered her slowly because she was tight as fuck. Major hadn't ever been with a virgin, but Kiyah damn sure felt like one. He was in heaven before he was all the way in. She scratched his back, crying out sinfully as he adjusted himself. He hoped that she was okay because there was no way he could stop at that point. After a few short powerful strokes, her body finally relaxed, and she daringly wrapped her other leg around him. Challenged accepted, Major pressed her back up against the wall and made sweet and obscene love to her. He hadn't ever felt that good being inside of a woman before. He was pissed off because he felt himself ready to nut, and he wasn't ready for it to end. In attempt to savor the moment, he slowed down, pushing her higher up the wall, coming face to face with her glistening pussy, and getting a healthy taste before bringing her back down on his stiff dick, slow grinding again to prevent early ejaculation. But when Kiyah whispered *don't stop*, so who was he to stop?

With Kiyah's encouragement, Major took his stroke game to a whole other level. He felt like he was having an outer body experience because he had never made love to a woman like he was fucking Kiyah. This was some epic shit, and his thug ass felt like crying because the shit was so good. He felt her legs shaking and knew that she was cumming. Tightening her grip around him, Kiyah cried out as happy tears flowed freely out the side of her eyes. Even though he wanted to, Major hurried up and pulled out of her warm delicacy to keep from shooting his kids inside of her.

"Got damn girl... you better not give my pussy to *no muthafuckin' body!* You hear me?" he asked and was dead ass serious.

Kiyah laughed, but when he gave her a look, she happily agreed and gave him a chaste kiss. But then, she retaliated with her own demand. "And this dick has *my* name written on it, and *no muthafuckin' body* can fuck with my dick. Do you hear me?" she countered.

"Damn straight baby." After basically agreeing to be exclusive, they washed each other off and then went to bed in the nude. That sex game hit different when you're fucking someone that you really fucks with. Kiyah and Major learned that night exactly why the song said, "good lovin' will make you cry."

❧ 17 ❧

Mercedes couldn't even bring herself to look at Duke, who still sat with an evil ass expression covering his handsome face. It had been a few hours since he'd picked her and Baby J up from off the street. After the big blow up in his car, she didn't know whether or not she should follow him inside. The way he'd snapped on her almost had her scared, but even without fully knowing him, she could tell that he was nothing like Maine. His anger stemmed from his worry, and it had taken her all of ten minutes to realize that before she got her ass out and crept into the house. When she got the nerve to finally follow him and her son's voices, she had found him in the kitchen helping Baby J eat a bowl of cereal. Without looking up, he nodded at the space across the island from them at a bowl he had prepared for her like he just knew she was going to come right in after him. Despite the fucked up situation she found herself in, Mercedes couldn't help the warm feeling in her stomach at his gesture, with his non cooking ass. After they all ate in silence, Duke gave her a pair of his sister's sweats since her and Mercedes were close in size and sent her to take a shower.

And there they sat. It was hours later and he had yet to say anything as he sat on the couch and watched TV with her baby, who was acting like he'd known Duke all of his little life. Unsure of what to say, she gazed around the room, taking in how nice the set up was. It looked completely different from the first time that she'd come over, and she wondered if the smoke gray furniture and blue décor was from a woman's touch or from Duke's. Jealousy hit her quickly, even though she had no room to be upset, she still felt some type of way about any female other than his sister being inside of their home.

"Stop staring at me unless you gone open yo mouth and tell me what I want to know." Duke said, never taking his eyes off of the TV. Quickly, Mercedes looked down at her hands. She couldn't bring herself to tell him about her situation with Maine. It was for lack of a better word *embarrassing*, especially what that nigga had put her out for. Mercedes was ashamed of the fact that after everything she'd put up with to give her son what she never had, which was a two parent household, Maine had betrayed her.

At first glance, the picture that Kiyah had sent to her was innocent enough. She too felt like everyone had a twin, so when she saw the little boy who favored her son, she was going to coo over him with Kiyah like women do; but a closer look had her narrowing her eyes in thought. The boy's mother, who was sitting right next to him, caught her attention and she felt sick. Even without her being as clear as her son, Mercedes could still see that it was a hoe named Aisha that Maine had cheated on her with more times than she could count.

The year that Baby J was born, that bitch had stayed running her mouth and Mercedes never had a problem shutting it, but that never stopped Maine from fucking with her. For months, they went back and forth with each other until Aisha just disappeared off the face of the earth. Mercedes had always figured that she finally got the hint and went and got a man of her own; but it would kill her to know that he'd really put her in hiding so that she could safely have his son. Because there was no way Aisha would have been able to walk the same streets as Mercedes, knowing she was pregnant without fucking her up.

Mercedes had waited up for Maine for hours to confront him, but she'd finally succumbed to sleep before he got there. That didn't stop her from waking up to the bullshit though. Like her body knew that nigga was about to cut up, Mercedes jumped out of her sleep, and before she even brushed her teeth, she was mushing him in the head while simultaneously putting the phone in his face and questioning him. He let her get off a few licks but that was it. Without answering any of her questions, he smacked her ass a few times and accused Baby J of not being his, which she thought was stupid considering that he'd forced her to take a paternity test at the hospital after she had him. She didn't even have time to argue back because he'd worked himself up that fast and was pulling her out the house and slamming the door. Not even five minutes later, he returned with their son and damn near threw him into her arms before giving her an evil glare and closing the door on them both.

That had been so early that morning that Mercedes sat there looking stupid and thinking that he would eventually let her back in, but that thought was quickly put to rest when she watched him pull his BMW out of the garage and peeled off. Again, she hopefully waited, just knowing that he would come back and let them inside. When she finally realized that she was on her own, she began walking, thinking that maybe Dreka could help or at least let her get a phone to call Kiyah. But that plan got shut down when Duke pulled his mad ass up.

After having been beyond mortified with everything that had transpired that morning, Mercedes couldn't take being further embarrassed by telling him exactly what happened. Especially when he was already fuming.

"You want some juice lil man?" His voice brought Mercedes out of her thoughts and she felt a flutter in her stomach at how sweet he was with Baby J, even though he was being an asshole to her. She silently watched him get up, admiring his slim athletic frame for a second before he disappeared into the kitchen. Figuring that the least she could do was thank him, she slid up from where she sat and followed him.

"So when was you gone tell me that you over there getting beat like a fuckin' piñata?" Duke sensed her behind him and asked without turning around. Mercedes sucked her teeth, instantly irritated.

"How do you expect me to want to talk to you when you keep saying rude shit to me?"

"How you expect me to trust you when you can't even keep shit a bill?" He countered, finally facing her.

"Okay, and how exactly was I supposed to bring it up? Oh yeah, by the way Duke, my baby daddy loves using me as a punching bag, but I stay so that my son can have a father and because I don't have shit to offer him on my own. That sounds like a great conversation starter." She tried to keep her voice down but what he was wanting from her was ridiculous. There were things that he'd kept from her in order to protect himself and she understood that, but he couldn't seem to give her the same respect.

"You coulda did that! We talk everyday shorty and you tell me everything else!" He snapped, coming around the island that separated them and getting in her face. "You know what I think? I think yo ass was scared to tell me because you knew what I was gone do, and deep down, you really still love that nigga too much to let something happen to him." Duke stood so close to her that she had to crane her neck to look up at him and the way his eyes darkened had her inching backwards. The truth of the matter was that she wasn't sure exactly why she chose to not tell him. Of course she was embarrassed, and it could have been a little bit of what he said too. She hated Maine most days, but she couldn't deny that there was some type of love still there. He was her child's father and they'd been together for a long time. He couldn't blame her for her feelings though.

"So, I'm wrong for not wanting something to happen to my son's father? You can't blame me for caring about somebody."

"The hell I can't! If you care more about *him* than *your own well being*, then that's a problem! I can't fuck with nobody who more worried bout a fuck nigga than themselves." He grit with disappointment covering his face.

"That's exactly what I need from you, a guilt trip! You didn't even have to stop earlier. I coulda just went to Kiyah's... matter fact, just take me there and you won't even have to worry about me and my problems!" Mercedes fumed and stormed off to grab her baby. Duke had a whole lot to say for someone she'd just met, and she wasn't in the mood to hear it whether it was the truth or not. He came out a minute later as she stood at the door with Baby J. Without saying a word to her, Duke snatched his keys off of the hook they were hanging on and opened the door so that she could step out first.

Once they were in the car, he skirted away from the house, barely giving her a chance to put on her seatbelt. He obviously was one of those drivers that liked to go fast when he was in a mood because he was speeding through the streets. It was either that or he was in a rush to get rid of her. After a while, she realized that they weren't even going in the direction of Kiyah's, and when they pulled up to The Marriott, she turned to him confused.

"Your best friend's crib gone be the first place that nigga look. I don't know what exactly you plan on doing but at least stay a couple days and get yo mind right." As bad as Mercedes wanted to, she couldn't argue because she knew Maine would without a doubt check Kiyah's apartment for her. So instead of saying anything smart, she merely nodded and allowed him to book her a room for three days. After Duke finally got her settled in and shoving some money into her hand, he left her alone, and as soon as he was gone, she was missing him.

❧ 18 ❧

Duke angrily drove away from the hotel and tried to calm himself down. That wasn't even his fight and yet he wanted to make it his. When he saw Mercedes walking down that driveway, he was honestly crushed. There was no way that the only person who'd caught his attention in a long time was getting beat on by her man and hadn't taken any steps to escape. He could understand her wanting to provide a father to her son and he could even believe that she was scared to leave due to finances; but there were women doing that shit every day. All of the assistance programs for women in Atlanta-- the world even-- Mercedes could have sought out some type of help, and since she hadn't, he was inclined to believe that she hadn't left because she ain't want to. Not one time had she listed fear as a reason that she'd stayed, so she couldn't have been scared of the nigga. Duke hadn't seen him since he'd moved in, but he could bet that her baby daddy wasn't even a real threat. He was probably a scrawny ass dude that wouldn't even fight a man but felt the need to lay hands on Mercedes' little defenseless ass. The thought alone had him pulling up to Mercedes' house instead of his own once he made it to their neighborhood. Of course he didn't see a car there besides her little ugly ass Honda, but that didn't stop him from

84

getting out and banging on the front door, just hoping that the nigga answered.

"Fuck am I even doin'?" He questioned himself after no one came ten minutes later. There he was about to start some shit over a girl he hadn't even piped yet. Shaking his head, he got back into his car, giving the house one last glance before going to his own.

"Hey you talked to Mercedes today? I been calling her and not getting an answer." Was the first thing out of Dreka's mouth the minute he stepped inside. As usual, she was lounging on the couch and flipping through channels. He wanted to ask her ass where she'd been this morning, but instead addressed the fact that she'd asked him about Mercedes.

"How you figure I know how to get in touch with shorty?" He frowned as he came into the room fully and moved her feet off the couch so that he could sit down.

"Cause you like *shorty,* plus I know you got her number that day, and y'all been caking... you ain't gotta front for me big bro." She said with a roll of her eyes.

"Nosey ass." He cracked a smile, but then it quickly disappeared at the thought of Mercedes. "I saw her earlier tho, her damn nigga been putting his hands on her and shit. Put her and her shorty out this morning. I just got back from getting her simple ass a room." Dreka's mouth dropped lower with every word that he said before she set her lips in a grim line.

"I *knew* he wasn't shit! And don't call her simple Duke, the girl's obviously going through it!" She pinched his arm and gave him an evil look.

"Yeah well, she goin' through it because she want to! She could have come to me or you for help but she didn't! The only reason she away from that nigga now is because I snatched her up as soon as I saw her walking outside with no shoes on and barely any clothes this morning! Did you even know her ass lived next door?" Duke fumed, causing a surprised expression to cover his sister's face.

"Oh damn! *She's* the girl from next door. No wonder she acts like that, her nigga over there hitting her for sport! We gotta help her Dookie!"

"Did you not just hear what I said?" Now he was irritated with his sister's slow ass too. He'd tried to help Mercedes, but the most that she'd let him do was take them to a room. As much as he fucked with her, he couldn't force her to do something that she didn't want to, and even if he could make her leave that nigga, chances were she'd go right back.

"So what she didn't come to us before! She probably didn't feel like she knew us well enough to be pouring out her heart to us! And look at how you're acting... I wouldn't have told you shit either if I was her! What room is she in? I'll go over there, I know she don't wanna be alone right now." Dreka stood and slipped her feet into her UGG house shoes then stomped off before he could even tell her the room number.

Duke continued to sit there for a few minutes, staring blankly at the TV screen as his sister's words replayed in his mind. He wondered if maybe he had been too hard on Mercedes. She was young and a mother of a young son. Maybe she had felt that dealing with her dude was the best she could do. Shit, from what she *had* told him, she'd been messing with her baby daddy for a few years.

Suddenly, Duke felt bad about how he had come at her. She'd already just gone through some shit and immediately after being helped by somewhat of a stranger, she was treated badly again. That wasn't the impression that he was trying to make on her; if anything, he wanted Mercedes to come to him if she needed something, so he'd have to make an effort to make her feel more comfortable. He'd felt like he'd had that covered, but after snapping on her the way he did, he would probably have to damn near start over. After everything that had gone down that day, Duke figured that he would give her a little time to cool down; even though he'd somewhat gotten over what had occurred, he didn't think she had. In fact, he was sure that on top of all the other shit Mercedes had on her mind, his judgmental comments had only added to the problem. Instead, he went ahead and scheduled her a spa day that he planned on having Dreka take her to and then he dialed up an old friend of the family that he knew would help her out.

Major's OG used to donate and do community service at a lot of women's shelters back when he'd stayed out in Atlanta, and she often dragged them all along to help out. Duke remembered Ms. Jones, the lady that ran the program, was always cool as hell; and as far as he knew, she still was running things over there.

As soon as she answered in her chipper voice, Duke gave her the run down on Mercedes and set up a time for the two to meet. He didn't plan to make her stay *in* the shelter, but he could definitely hook her up with Ms. Jones so that she could put her up on game and eventually have her able to take care of herself and her son. By the time Dreka came running down the stairs with a huge duffle bag, he was off the phone and had handled everything.

"She in room 2208." Duke informed without looking away from the TV. He heard his sister huff and knew that she was probably pouting or giving him an evil glare, but he wasn't worried about her whiny ass.

"You not gone come with me?"

"Nope. I just left from up there and I know she good, besides she need time to cool off." He shrugged. Duke had done all that he could do that day, but best believe, he planned to be up there bright and early the next morning, so he could get her ready for the change that was coming. Dreka stormed out and he quickly sent her a text of the details for their spa day before settling back in to watch ESPN.

❧ 19 ❧

E ven though it was spur of the moment and started out for a bad cause, Cali turned out to be everything plus more for Kiyah. She clicked with Major's family, he took her shopping and bought her more than she wanted, and the sex was phenomenal. Kiyah couldn't wait to get back home and fill her girl in on everything. She had texted her but didn't get a reply, which was normal for Mercedes at times so it didn't bother Kiyah. Major said his goodbyes to his people and Kiyah followed suit. She had even exchanged numbers with Yanna, which was surprising to Major because his sister didn't like anybody, just like his mom.

Kiyah felt like she was on cloud nine as her and Major prepared for takeoff. She could get used to skipping lines at the airport and shit. Once they were settled, Major took time to handle some business, so Kiyah utilized that time to pull up some study notes on her phone. After studying for a little over an hour, she drifted off to sleep. Major shook her awake after they landed and Kiyah stretched her legs before getting up.

"You was knocked out... slobbin' and shit! But you cute when you sleep."

"I was not slobbin'," Kiyah wiped her mouth just to make sure.

"You even snore, but it's a cute lil snore though, so it's all good," Major continued to tease her.

Kiyah laughed and playfully punched him. They both got up and Major's truck was right where he left it. Once they were settled inside, Major asked her what she wanted to eat, and she told him that he could swoop through Chick-fil-A since she had a taste for a spicy chicken sandwich.

"A woman who knows what she wants to eat... yeeahhh, you one of a kind girl."

"You just got all kinda jokes today huh?" Kiyah playfully rolled her eyes.

Kiyah had already emailed her instructor for the one class she had, so once she made it home, she planned to clean up a little and then get up with her girl Mercedes. Major ordered their food and Kiyah whispered for him to add some buffalo spice to it. She loved dipping her fries in that sauce. Once he paid and got their food, she wasted no time digging in. Her phone vibrated and before checking the text, Kiyah noticed that it was almost eleven thirty. Even though she had slept the whole flight, she was still a little tired.

Chris: You okay? You normally don't miss class.

Kiyah: Yeah I'm fine. I emailed my excuse. Thanks for checking on me.

Chris: Always. We still on for our last study session next week?

Kiyah: Yep. We gonna go out with a bang.

Kiyah sent that last text and put her phone back down so she could eat.

"Don't get that lil nerd ass nigga fucked up."

After Major said that, Kiyah busted out laughing.

"Boy, if you don't stop. Me and him only study together. Ion even look at him like that," she dipped another fry and ate it.

"I'm just saying... he look like the nerd version of..."

Major's phone rang so he cut his sentence off and answered. Kiyah knew that it was his mom by the direction of the conversation. She tuned Major out and continued eating her food.

"Ma said she can't wait to see you again," Major told her after he hung up.

"Aww... I can't wait either. Your family is so cool," Kiyah admitted.

She wanted to say more, but she kept it to herself. Deep down, she somewhat knew that her parents wouldn't be as receptive to Major as his parents were to her, but time would tell because they would be there in two weeks. Kiyah finished off her food just as Major pulled into her complex.

"What you getting into today?" Kiyah asked him as they got out and gathered all of her bags.

"Just gotta handle some business... then I'll probably slide back through if you up for it."

"Of course I am... I just gotta check on Mercedes. I can't allow her to get too distant. She got a lot going on," Kiyah said and then her phone rang.

"Girl you gon' live a long time... I was just talking about you," Kiyah smiled after she answered Mercedes call.

"What's wrong?" Kiyah dropped her smile and asked after she heard her friend sniffling.

"Maine beat me again and put me out... then..."

"WHAT? Where are you?" Kiyah cut her off and started back walking towards her door.

"Duke got me a hotel room... I'm okay for now..."

"Duke? Wait Mercedes, you taking me too..."

"WHAT THE FUCK?" Kiyah yelled when she noticed her door had been kicked in.

"Wait right here!" Major told her and made his way inside the apartment.

"What happened? What's going on?" Mercedes became worried on the other end of the phone.

"Let me call you right back girl. Somebody done broke into my apartment," Kiyah ended the call before she could hear what Mercedes was about to say.

Major was taking too long and Kiyah was getting impatient. She tried to wait, but ended up going inside anyway. A lamp was knocked over, but other than that, she didn't see anything out of place in the living room.

"Don't look like nobody took shit and ain't nobody in this mu'fucka," Major appeared from the back, tucking his gun back into his waist.

"That's crazy as hell. No one has ever broken in before. I wonder..." she stopped midsentence and it hit her.

"Maine must have thought Mercedes was here. That punk ass nigga," Kiyah fumed.

"Maine? What Maine?" Major asked.

"Mercedes' stupid ass baby daddy. She just told me he put her out. It had to be him. Who the fuck else would break in and not take shit?" Kiyah was pissed the fuck off.

She saw Major pacing the floor before he pulled his phone out and made a phone call. He was pissed off and so was she. Kiyah went and grabbed the broom so that she could sweep the glass up from the lamp.

"I gotta go holla at Duke. That nigga Maine work for us and my homie Duke been seeing your girl. He gon' flip the fuck out when I tell him the rest of the story. Put the chain on the door and I'll call you in a few," Major instructed.

Kiyah locked the door behind him and was left standing there looking dumbfounded. She would have never thought that her and Mercedes would end up connected to friends and how crazy was it that Maine worked for them. It was a small ass world, but Kiyah couldn't help but to think that someone was playing with fire. She just hoped that the wrong people didn't get burned.

20

Major hopped in his truck and left Kiyah's apartment complex with the quickness. He had to holla at Duke and see where he was so that he could talk to him face to face. The world was just too fuckin' small, and he knew that it was about to get smaller if Duke had his way once he revealed the rest of the information to him. Twenty minutes later, Major pulled up to one of their low-key spots and Duke's car was already there. He parked his truck beside his homie's and got out. Major sent Kiyah a text as he made his way to the door to make sure that she was okay, and she replied back instantly, letting him know that everything was all good but she was going to visit with Mercedes shortly.

As soon as Major walked in, he spotted Duke with a Corona in his hand. He closed the door and thought about going to get a drink, but quickly decided against it because he knew that they weren't going to be there long.

"So what's up wit you and Mercedes? You feeling her like for real for real?" Major pried.

"Yeah I'm feeling shawty, but I can tell she damaged. She flipped out on me and all I was tryna do was help her ass. Say yo, Kiyah is her best friend though?"

"Yeah... small world, but you ain't gon' believe the rest of what I found out."

"Aww hell.... I can tell this bout to be some shit just by the look on your face. Let me go grab a shot for this," Duke disappeared to the kitchen.

He reappeared with a Hennessey bottle that had a corner of liquor in it. Duke wasted no time throwing it back and motioning with his hands for Major to continue on with what he had to say.

"Bruh... that nigga Maine is Mercedes' baby daddy!" Major finally confessed the news that Kiyah told him.

"WHAT THE FUCK?" Duke jumped up and fumed.

Major watched as his boy paced the floor deep in thought. If Major had to guess, he figured that Duke was thinking about conversations that he must have had with Mercedes and piecing shit together for himself.

"That nigga a woman beater... and that punk as mu'fucka lives right beside me. I'ma beat his muthafuckin' ass!" Duke grabbed his phone and keys and prepared to leave.

"Wait man... we gotta think things through," Major grabbed his arm.

"Fuck that nigga!" Duke snatched away and left out of the door while talking cash money shit about Maine.

Major had no choice but to follow Duke to keep him from doing something crazy. By the time he made it out of the door, Duke was jumping in his car. It was Monday, so Maine had to be out East. He jumped in his truck and headed in that direction. Duke was breaking all kinda laws, and Major prayed that he didn't get stopped because they didn't need that unnecessary attention. He could see Duke a few cars in front of him, but when he got caught at a light that Duke ran, he was stuck. Major tapped the steering wheel as he impatiently waited for the light to change. He called Duke two times, all to no avail.

By the time Major made it to the spot, Duke was already there of course and by the way he was parked, it was clear that he pulled up in a hurry and hopped straight out. Major hurriedly parked and made his way inside. Maine was on the floor with blood spilling out of his nose, and it appeared that his right eye was swollen shut. Duke reached for his gun, and Major snatched it from him before he could take it off safety. Maine was on the floor coughing and rolling from side to side. Duke had whooped his ass in a short period of time, but it looked like the nigga had been jumped by a gang of at least six.

"Come on man... it ain't even worth all this. Get outta here and go calm down," Major instructed his boy.

When Duke was gone, Major stared down at Maine in disgust. He couldn't believe that the nigga was out there beating women, his own baby's mother to be more specific. If Duke would have had his way, Maine would have been dead a long time ago, but Major had a soft spot for him because of the work that he had put in. He knew there was no room for soft spots in the game, so it was time for them to part ways. Major just hoped that Maine wouldn't make him have to put a bullet in his dome.

"After this month, we done with business on all levels. You need to take some time to get yo shit together man. The only reason you still breathing is because of the history we got together, but don't make me regret that shit," Major groused and left Maine laying on the floor.

❧ 21 ❧

"**D**amnnnn boy... they fucked you up!" Petey covered his mouth with a fist as he inspected Maine's injuries.

"Fuck you nigga! And fuck them too!" Maine grumbled bitterly. He wanted to slap his ass upside the head, but knew that he couldn't move as quickly as he wanted without getting a headache.

"What was this all about?" Chris, who'd come in with Petey, asked calmly after he took a seat next to Maine on the couch.

"A *dead* bitch, but that's beside the point. I called y'all niggas over here so that I could tell y'all that we moving the plan up." Maine didn't even want to think about how Mercedes could have even known Duke and Major. The thought of her being in either one of those niggas' presence was enough to have him tearing up his mama living room. When Duke first busted in the house, he thought that somehow he'd found out about Maine skimming their product, but he quickly learned that it had nothing to do with that. The first words out his mouth were something about "putting his hands on Mercedes" and from there it was on. Duke had beaten his ass so bad that he had to lie and say it was more than one person who'd inflicted his injuries so that he wouldn't look like a total bitch. Then to top it all off, Major had cut him out completely! His money was already low from having to work in the houses, but now his shit was going to be completely dried up.

Maine couldn't even believe that Major would care that much about what *he* did with *his* bitch. Not to the point that he'd stop him from making money, but since he had, it was time to put their plan into action. Him and Chris had talked explicitly about robbing the trap that they both worked at. They were going to team up with the Get Low boys and take Major down. Little did either Chris or Petey know, but Maine already had an "in" with them niggas. His other baby's mama, Aisha, was directly linked with them, due to her older brother running the crew. He'd already talked to his ass about the transition and was a part of them burning down one of Major's traps. That had been a warning, but obviously the nigga didn't take heed to those.

When Maine realized that he hadn't gotten a reaction out of Chris or Petey, he looked between the two of them, noticing the doubt on their faces.

"What, y'all niggas scared?" He barked, instantly getting agitated.

"I ain't scared, you already know I'm down for the cause, but it's only the three of us. How the fuck we sposed to get anywhere near the trap especially when niggas know that you blacklisted?" Petey said unsure. He hadn't been privy to the whole plan or even Maine's dealings with the Get Low Boys. As far as he knew, it would just be them going up against a house full of ruthless little niggas and he didn't think the odds were good. The shit Maine was talking about doing was a suicide mission and he valued his life.

"If you done sounding like a lil bitch nigga, I got back up for us and don't even worry about how we gone get in... I got that covered too. That's why I'm the brains." Maine took his eyes off of Petey, who seemed satisfied with his answer and turned to Chris. "Now what's yo problem?"

"I don't got a problem, and I'm damn sure not afraid. I was just thinking bout some other shit." Chris said, sitting back in the chair he was in and resting his elbows on the arms. The plastic that Maine's mama had covering every stitch of her furniture had all of their asses sticking to it. After staring him down for a minute, Maine decided to let the shit go. Whatever Chris' issue was, it would come to light at some point, and Maine wouldn't hesitate to put a bullet in his head.

"Well since that's all taken care of, can we figure out what day we gone do this? Y'all niggas still work for them so figure out when the house will be the weakest and we'll go from there, cause shorty ain't gone just be able to help whenever. She's gonna need a day and time." Maine explained, talking about Aisha. He'd already figured out that the best way to get a young nigga distracted was with some pussy and who better than his thick ass baby mama. Aisha was the hood thot, and everybody knew her, but what they didn't know was that he was her baby's daddy. Everybody assumed that she didn't know who her kid's daddy was and he wanted to keep it that way for more reasons than one. He had been trying to keep Mercedes from ever finding out and had done a good job of keeping the two apart, but Kiyah's meddlesome ass just had to ruin things for him by showing her that picture. If he could, he'd smack that hoe too, but unlike Mercedes, Kiyah wasn't scared to go toe-to-toe with him and had done so a few times. He should have beaten Mercedes' ass for her friend being so damn nosy, but it was too late now. She was long gone or at the least under the protection of Duke and Major, but Maine would worry about that some other time. Atlanta was only but so big and eventually, he would catch up to his baby mama. But until then, he would work on his take over.

❦ 2 2 ❦

Even though Duke had been a complete asshole, at the same time, Mercedes couldn't deny that he was also a Godsend. Not only had he tucked her away safely, but he'd paid for her to get royal treatment at a spa and hooked her up with a lady by the name of Ms. Jones. The first day that she had met with her, Mercedes had been embarrassed as hell. This was the third stranger that was privy to her damn personal business, so right away she had an attitude until Kiyah nipped that shit in the bud. She quickly told her friend, *"Bitch, this lady ain't your problem,* **your baby daddy** *that can't keep his hands to himself is! Let her help you!"* As hard as it was to hear that, Mercedes knew it was the truth. She had to stop allowing the embarrassment of her situation to keep her from seeking out help.

Not even a week later, Ms. Jones had gotten her enrolled in a Cosmetology course, Baby J was in a daycare that catered to mothers working or going to school, and she had her on the waiting list for a low income apartment. At first, Mercedes was nervous about school and possibly running into Maine. She looked over her shoulder every day, thinking that he would be coming after her and Baby J. It was honestly hard for her to relax considering that she didn't know when or how he was going to come because she was sure he was coming for them. Thankfully, he had yet to learn their whereabouts and she hoped that he never would, but Mercedes knew that was wishful thinking.

"I hope you ain't cooped up in here thinking bout that nigga!" Duke's voice sounded as he entered her hotel room, bringing Mercedes out of her thoughts. He swept into the room looking just as good as ever in a white Adidas t-shirt, black Gucci jeans held up by a Hermès belt, and some classic Adidas on his feet. Mercedes took him in from head to toe and a shudder rippled through her body. She quickly recovered and attempted to fix her face into an annoyed scowl before he caught the fact that she was thinking about taking off his clothes.

"I wasn't thinking about Maine." She lied. "Contrary to what you think, I didn't enjoy getting my ass beat every day!" No matter how sweet Duke was, every since he'd found out about who and what was going on in her life, he made it a point to irritate her about it. If he wasn't talking shit about Maine then he was clowning her for thinking about him. Mercedes rolled her eyes and attempted to brush past him but he snatched her right back.

"My bad, I ain't tryna piss you off or come down on your head. I just don't want you to be considering going back to that nigga. I know how y'all females are and you think way more with your heart than you do with your head. You need to understand that with a nigga who puts his hands on you, thinking with your heart can get you killed. I'm just tryna prevent that because I care about you and lil man."

Duke brought his hand up and caressed her cheek as he stared down into her eyes. Without thinking, Mercedes closed the distance between them and planted a kiss on his lips. He stilled but not even a second later, Duke was invading her mouth with his tongue as his hands roamed her body. He'd been trying to be cool about his feelings for her and simply be a listening ear and a friend to her, but the minute that Mercedes invited him to kiss her, all of his resolve went away. He wanted her to be *his*, and if he could, he'd kill Maine just to make that happen, but he knew that wasn't something she wanted done.

Mercedes moaned as Duke firmly gripped her ass, ready to allow him entry into her body. She'd completely forgotten about Duke being there to take her to school. If she had things her way, she'd just stay there with him and say fuck leaving her room. She was so into the kiss and the feel of his body against hers that the sound of his phone ringing went unnoticed.... by her anyway. The insistent ringing had him pulling away from her, but he didn't answer; instead, he cut off the ringer and took a step back.

"Damn, we supposed to been left." He ran a hand down his waves and avoided meeting her eyes as she stood there panting. Mercedes could tell that the moment was gone, and she wanted to throw that damn phone out of the window. She was sexually frustrated and in need of some dick, preferably *Duke's dick*, but from the way he was acting, she knew it wouldn't be that day. With a roll of her eyes, she moved to retrieve her cosmetology bag from the couch and then followed Duke, who was already standing at the door, out into the hall.

The ride down to his car was silent. Mercedes couldn't help but wonder if it was because he regretted kissing her, but she was way too scared to ask. She walked behind him through the lobby, irritated that they'd been interrupted and by the amount of women ogling him as they walked past. It instantly had her in an even more foul mood, and she made sure to let him know when he finally addressed her once they were in his car and driving away.

"You wanna stop and grab something to eat real quick? You still got like a half hour til yo class start." He mused, glancing her way.

"Naw I'm good." She replied dryly, not bothering to turn away from the window. She could see him out of the corner of her eye still looking at her before shaking his head and returning his attention to the street ahead. It was moments like the one back at the hotel room that made her feel insecure about her past. Mercedes didn't know whether or not Duke wanted her. Sometimes his actions and words said he did and sometimes he gave her a completely different vibe. As bad as she wanted him, she also had a lot of shit going on and trying to figure out his feelings really wasn't something she had time for.

She'd started school, was working on her image on social media, and was in the beginning stages of making a beauty and hair channel on YouTube in addition to hiding from her deranged baby daddy, so fitting a confused man into the equation-- even if he was fine-- just didn't work for her.

"Don't worry about picking me up. I'm doin' somebody's hair later so she's gonna give me a ride." Mercedes told him stiffly as soon as the car stopped in front of her school. She hurried to open the door and got out before he could say anything and was glad when he didn't try to stop her.

❦

"GIRRRRL, I'M SO GLAD YOU COULD COME AND TIGHTEN ME UP." Raina exclaimed hours later as she led Mercedes into her apartment.

"No problem anything for the girl who got me poppin' on Instagram." Mercedes teased with a chuckle. She was serious though. Due to Raina, she had a small clientele and had been pulling in more money. If she kept it up, she wouldn't even need to move into the low income apartments that Ms. Jones had signed her up for; she could get a much better apartment in a better neighborhood too.

"Well shit, there's definitely more where that came from. Them heffas down at the club stay askin' bout who do my hair. For them to make so much money, you'd be surprised how cheap them hoes is, but I definitely dropped your name and told them how reasonable your prices are." Raina stopped at the table that was behind her couch and sat in one of the chairs, still texting away on her phone as she spoke.

"Well send them my way, I ain't turning down no coins!" Mercedes meant that too. She needed all her coins and she was sure that once she got her license, things would be even better.

"Okay. I'm goin' in tonight so I'll pass on your info."

Mercedes got started tightening the tracks that rested in Raina's head as Queen's station on Pandora played in the background. She focused on her task, barely noticing Raina's huffing and puffing, even though it was obvious the girl wanted her attention. Finally, after she sighed heavily for like the twentieth time, Mercedes gave in.

"What's got you all worked up girl? You been blowing since I got here." Mercedes asked, although she really didn't care. They were cool, but she wasn't a friend like how Kiyah was.

"My bad! It's just this nigga Duke been tryna act funny like he don't fuck with me like that... when not too long ago, his ass was in my bed!" Raina spilled and immediately Mercedes stopped working on her head.

"Duke? He like your boyfriend or something?" Mercedes was almost scared to hear her answer. She held her breath, hoping that either they didn't have the same Duke or that she was mistaken.

"Yeah, he just moved back out here and baby that nigga is paid! We used to fuck around back in the day, so he hit me up when he came back tryna get that old thang back!" She giggled and danced in her seat, making Mercedes sick to her stomach. "We been fuckin' around heavy too, but his ass ain't been answering his phone all day. Nigga bouta make me pull up on his ass."

Mercedes tuned her out, not saying anything about the information she'd just heard. Now she understood why Duke was acting funny with her and she wondered if maybe it was Raina who had called him earlier and interrupted them. Of course, she couldn't ask her, but as soon as she saw Duke, she was going to get down to the bottom of why he was trying to play her for a fool.

23

In spite of all of the drama that had been unfolding, Kiyah was happy that her graduation day was almost there. She had one last final to take, and even though she was confident, she still decided to keep her word and meet up with Chris for a study date. She had met with the job as promised and would be moving very soon. Kiyah hadn't mentioned that detail to Major yet because it somewhat saddened her, but she had to stay focused. Moving an hour and some change away, depending on traffic, was going to be an adjustment because he normally popped up on her at any time to bring the most random things, mostly food. While on the way to the café, Kiyah's phone rang, and she slid the bar across, answering Chris' call.

"Hey Chris. I'm on my way now."

"Hey Kiyah. I was actually trying to catch you before you left home. Change of plans. My mom cooked this fabulous meal and brought it to me... it's so much food and I'd love to share, how about you come by my place?"

"Ummm.... I guess I can do that. I'm not one to pass up a home cooked meal," Kiyah laughed.

She had never been to his house, but figured it wouldn't hurt anything. Kiyah still felt a little bad about the time Major ran Chris off, but low-key, she was happy that he did. It was the beginning of some-thing special for the both of them.

"Great... I'll text you the address."

Kiyah ended the call and the text with the address came through shortly afterwards. She clicked on it and Siri notified her that the loca-tion was fifteen minutes away. Another phone call came through and Kiyah smiled as she answered it.

"Heeyyy girl! How are you?"

"Kiyaahhh! I'm so excited!" Mercedes bubbled.

"What happened girl?"

"Ever since Maine has been outta the picture, shit has just been looking up for me. Don't cut me off with the *I told you so's* either... let me finish."

Kiyah laughed while biting her tongue. Mercedes joined in and then continued with her story.

"So remember how you always told me to get in school for hair since I do it so well? I did... annndddd, I also started a channel on YouTube and I connected it to my other social media accounts and that shit seemed like it blew up overnight. Duke's sister shared it on her page, and I looked up and saw that Tiny and some other celebrities shared it too."

Kiyah was so proud of her friend. She had been through so much and she truly deserved the happiness that she was receiving.

"I'm sooo happy for you Mercedes. You just don't know. This is such a blessing that you really deserve. I'll be sure to share it on my pages after I stop driving. You been moving in silence..."

"Yes girl... I was so scared and I literally didn't expect it to take off so fast, but..."

"But what?"

"I can't help but to feel like Maine is gonna pop up and snatch all of my happiness away. This shit seems too good to be true," Mercedes sighed.

"Fuck Maine!! You enjoy everything that's happening for you and Baby J and forget about him. Trust Duke to protect you. I can tell he cares for you more than a little bit," Kiyah disclosed.

"Hmm... you're right, but anyways... are you ready for Friday?" Mercedes changed the subject.

"Yeesss... but I'm nervous about my parents meeting Major. There won't be an in between, they're either gonna love him or hate him."

"We both know your parents are strict, but you're grown. Major makes you so happy and I'm happy for you. I hope they like him because I know you'll feel conflicted if they don't."

"I hope so too girl... I hope so too," Kiyah mumbled.

"Well girl, it looks like I've just about reached my destination... let me find out what number Chris lives in."

"Chris done got you to his house? He seems like a psycho so be careful," Mercedes warned.

"Chris is just a little nerd, I'll be alright. I'll call you back later though."

Kiyah ended the call and sent Chris a text. While she waited for him to reply, she did just what she promised Mercedes she would do: went on her page and shared her channel. She was impressed with the hits she had received and had faith that the numbers would triple by the end of the week. Chris hit her back and then Kiyah grabbed her backpack and got out. The weather was nice and warm. Kiyah had on a pair of blue jean shorts, a red Nike shirt, and a pair of black and red Vapormax. She made it to Chris' door and got ready to knock, but he opened it before she had a chance to.

"Come on in," he smiled.

"It smells good in here," Kiyah smelled the aroma of food instantly and her stomach began doing flips. She silently hoped that it was as good as it smelled.

"My mom can really cook. I'm sure you'll love it."

For the first time ever, Kiyah noticed that Chris had a little swag to him. She wondered if it had always been there and she just never noticed or if it was something he had recently developed. He seemed different to her and she couldn't figure out when the change came about.

"You wanna eat or study first?"

"I wanna say eat, but we better study because I might eat and get sleepy," Kiyah laughed, but she was dead ass serious.

"That wouldn't be so bad," Chris mumbled, but Kiyah heard him loud and clear. He tried to clean it up right away.

"We can study for about thirty minutes, eat while it's still hot, and then study some more. How about that?"

"That's fine," Kiyah conceded and sat down at the table, ignoring his first comment.

They dove right into their studying session. Kiyah started out quizzing Chris, and when he missed a couple of questions, she knew that something was wrong. It was clear that Chris liked her on a different level, and Kiyah knew if she pried too much, he might take it the wrong way. When he stumbled on another question, she couldn't hold it any longer.

"Are you okay Chris?"

"I think I'm just hungry," he lied.

"Well let's go ahead and eat," she suggested and got up.

Kiyah followed Chris into the kitchen and filled her plate with roast and potatoes, cabbage, and cornbread. If the food was as good as it smelled, she was about to be in for a treat. She sat back down at the table across from Chris and realized that she didn't get anything to drink.

"Some strawberry lemonade from Wendy's would be so fye with this, but I guess water is fine."

"I can go grab some. There's a Wendy's right down the street," Chris stood up.

"Oh nah Chris... you don't have to do that. I was just..."

"I'll be right back," Chris stated and left before Kiyah could protest any further.

Kiyah put a napkin over her plate so that she could wait on Chris to get back before eating. She got up and walked down the hall to find the bathroom. The first door on the right was closed, but she opened it and noticed that it looked like a closet or something. Just when she was about to close the door, something caught her attention. Kiyah pushed the door opened and flipped on the light switch and her mouth hit the floor. There were pictures of her all over the walls. Some pictures were of her and Chris together and she had never taken any pictures with him. Kiyah knew that Chris liked her, but she had no idea his ass was *obsessed* like that. She had to think fast. She turned to leave and was in for another shock when she saw a few pair of her panties hanging on the back of the door. Kiyah quickly exited the room, being sure to close the door, and she went and sat back down at the table. As soon as she was seated, Chris walked back through the front door smiling.

She was sick to her stomach, but Kiyah knew that she couldn't make any sudden moves. Honestly, she had lost her appetite, but she couldn't let on to anything or he would have known something was up.

"You okay?" he quizzed.

"Yeah," she quickly lied.

"You sure?"

"Well... my best friend just called and she's going through some shit. I didn't wanna bail out on you, but I do need to go and check on her," Kiyah put on her best act.

"You know what? Maybe we can just eat and then you can leave and check on her. We're both gonna ace this exam tomorrow anyway," Chris offered.

Kiyah agreed and they started eating. The food was actually good, but her nerves were shot. She was sitting across from a psycho, trying to act normal. Kiyah had watched enough Lifetime movies to know to be calm, not to mention the psychology classes she had taken. She was so happy once they were done eating, she damn near sprinted out of there after forcing herself to give Chris a hug. She made it to her car and got the hell away from there. While driving, another reality slapped her in the face-- it was *Chris* who broke into her apartment.

❧ 24 ❧

Major knew that Kiyah was excited about the day, and he had been planning for weeks on how he could make her day one that she would never forget. Even if he wanted to, Major couldn't forget the date May 3rd because it had been talked about so much. If he had met Kiyah sooner, she would already be his wife, but Major planned on making that happen in the future when the time was right. Kiyah rolled over and wrapped her arms around him and he started getting hard. It didn't take anything but a simple touch from her to turn him on.

"Hmmm... looks like my friend is awake," she began rubbing his dick.

"Don't start shit you can't finish," he warned.

"Baby you know I can finish anything I start," she smirked and disappeared under the covers.

You would think that they hadn't fucked each other's brains out the night before, but it was clear that neither of them could get enough. Kiyah swallowed him whole and Major's toes began to curl. He'd received some good head as well as good sex in his life, but Kiyah was the best of both worlds. She sucked, licked, and slurped his dick and balls and without warning, Kiyah was on top of him and easing down onto his stiffness.

"Damn bae," Major grunted as Kiyah glided up and down.

She rotated her pace; slow then fast, and back and forth. Major reached up and fondled her breasts and then he finally leaned up and sucked on them. The shit must have been feeling good to Kiyah because her legs began shaking and she screamed out, letting him know that she was about to come. After her orgasm ended, Major flipped her over and entered her from the back. She threw her ass back at him until he went too deep. When she tried to run, he gripped her around the waist and pulled her back to him. He gave her an A for effort on how she tried to take the dick, but he still had to show her who was in control.

"Stop... tryna run..." he pumped in and out of her.

"Boy... ain't nobo... ain't nobody running."

Major flipped her over again and put both of her legs over each shoulder. He went as deep as he could go for a few more minutes and was barely able to pull out in time, but he did and released his nut on her stomach.

"You got a long day ahead and look how you started it?" he fake fussed at her.

"Shit I started it out right," she giggled and got up, making her way to the bathroom.

Major had a full day planned for Kiyah and he couldn't wait to see her reaction to everything.

"Be ready in thirty minutes babe," he called out to her.

She replied and he pulled out his phone to make sure that everything was on schedule. Kiyah walked out of the bathroom with her towel wrapped around her and almost tempted Major to go for round two, but instead, he smacked her on the ass and went and hopped in the shower. Fifteen minutes later, he was out, dried off, and throwing on a pair of khaki shorts and a yellow Polo tee. He had quite a few clothes at Kiyah's place like he had been living there for a long ass time. Kiyah's phone rang. When she answered, he knew that it had to be Mercedes by the way she lit up. He had a full spa treatment scheduled for them. Since her friend did her hair the day before, that was one thing he didn't have to schedule but he did pay Mercedes and tipped her well.

"Baby, you got Mercedes pulling up in a limo? You so damn extra!" she giggled and grabbed her phone and purse and headed for the door.

Major was right behind her.

"Today is all about you. The driver has all of the instructions and I'll meet you in a few hours," he kissed her and locked the door behind him.

Once they made it outside, Mercedes was standing up through the sunroof with a bottle of champagne in her right hand. Kiyah did a light jog and made her way towards her awaiting ride and then hopped in. She blew Major a kiss and when they took off, so did he. He had a little business to handle, and he hoped there weren't any issues because he needed it to be a smooth Friday. Thirty minutes later, Major pulled up to one of the spots and parked beside one of the workers cars. He got out and made his way inside and spoke to the guys before going to the back where he found Bo counting money.

"I was just bout to call you... the money is good for this week, but when I went back and looked at the books for the past previous weeks, shit was off. The short end came from your boy, old boy or whatever the fuck he is," Bo explained.

Hearing that made Major regret letting Maine live. The nigga had turned out to be a fucking thief and a woman beater, both in which Major considered to be cowards. The nigga had been real quiet ever since Duke beat the fuck out of him, but Major knew there was a chance that he was somewhere plotting. He was hoping that Maine had bowed out gracefully, but hearing that the nigga had been stealing let Major know that there was about to be some smoke in the city. He chopped it up with Bo for a few more minute and then went and checked on a few other spots. Time was flying by and it was almost time for the next part of Major's surprise. He knew that Kiyah's parents would be in soon, so he planned to let her spend a little time with them before she had to leave for the ceremony. While in route to his next location, Major's phone rang and he answered it on Bluetooth.

"What's up Nisha?"

"Hey Major... how's it going?"

"Same ol' same ol'... you done dropped that load yet?" he quizzed.

"Any day now. Time really flew by."

"I can't believe you really bout to be a mom... you gone be a great one though, but shit still a shock," he confessed.

"Yeah... it's scary but it is what it is now. How's your lil relationship going?"

"Whooaaaa, the shade! Ain't that's how y'all females say it?" Major laughed.

"I was just asking... I know you, but listen..."

"Aye I gotta take this call Nish, I'ma hit you back," Major ended the call and answered Kiyah's FaceTime call.

"Babbeee, why am I at the Mercedes dealership?" she squealed.

"Damn, I was supposed to beat you there, but I'm taking the exit right now. Sit tight," he instructed and when she hung up, she was still screaming.

He pulled up to the dealership about five minutes later and saw Kiyah and Mercedes walking around. It was so crazy that she was standing in front of the black G-Wagon that he had purchased for her, snapping pictures. Major pulled up beside them and parked.

"You like that?" he asked after he got out.

"This is too fye!"

"Get in!" he told her after he heard the locks click.

Kiyah opened the door and hopped in the driver's seat. When her eyes landed on the steering wheel and she saw her name engraved on it, she jumped out of the driver's seat and ran up to Major and leaped into his arms.

"Oh my God... Oh my God!! I can't believe this!" Kiyah exclaimed as tears of joy formed into her eyes.

"This is only the beginning baby girl, this is only the beginning."

His boy came out and handed Kiyah her keys, and she jumped back into the drivers' seat and Mercedes hopped in on the passenger's side.

"Go meet up with your people and I'll see you later," he instructed and watched her drive away.

Major thanked his boy and then headed to his house so he could regroup before the night.

After Kiyah walked across the stage and took a million pictures,

Major confirmed their dinner reservations. She wanted Ruth Chris and he made it happen. His boy had even showed up to the graduation with Mercedes, and he had her baby more than she did. Duke was acting like he had been a dad forever, and although it was cute or what-ever, Major couldn't wait to clown his ass once they were alone. He officially met Kiyah's parents before graduation. They were cordial, but Major could tell that her dad had a little air in his chest. He hoped that he was wrong because he was feeling the hell out of Kiyah and he didn't want any static with her people.

They arrived at the restaurant on time. Kiyah drove her new whip and her parents were with her and Major was right behind. Once they made it inside, they were seated immediately in the area Major had set up for them. He pulled Kiyah's chair back and helped her get seated and then went to check on some more shit. When Major walked back into their space, he overheard Mr. Davis talking and he stopped in his tracks.

"Who the hell does he think he is? I can provide for my own daughter."

"Daddy... Major and I love each other so please chill out. You should be happy I found a man who loves and respects and can also buy me nice things."

"He's probably a drug dealer. I raised you better than this Kiyah Davis," her dad spat.

Major made his presence known so that they could end their little argument. He took his seat and stared straight into David's eyes.

"You raised a smart young lady and I do love her. I'm doing all of this because she deserves it, not to upstage anyone. That ain't even my style. I'm hoping that we can enjoy the rest of her special day without any problems," Major spoke as calm as he could.

He could tell by the look in her dad's eyes that the problems had just began. Major wasn't into disrespecting his seniors, but he didn't take disrespect either. He just knew that the night was going to get a little more interesting.

❧ 25 ❧

Mercedes had been waiting to confront Duke about the Raina situation but with Kiyah's graduation, her classes, and her new business ventures, it never seemed like the right time. Add to that the fact that him and Major had their own shit going on and it had been pretty much impossible to get his ass alone. At that point, she really wasn't sure if she was more upset that he was playing games with her or if it was because Raina had gotten something she wanted. Either way, she was pissed and as hard as she had tried to give Duke attitude to let him know, he obviously wasn't taking her seriously. Besides her personal issues though, Duke had been really looking out for her, and the relationship he had blossoming with Baby J was the cutest. The fact that he was stepping up and helping her with her son eased some of the guilt she felt about keeping him from his father.

"So you just gone keep actin' like ain't shit bothering you?" Duke asked after they'd been driving for a while. They'd taken Baby J to HippoHopp and he had jumped and played himself into a deep sleep. It was crazy to Mercedes how whenever she was with Duke, she didn't fear Maine running up on her. Ever since that day he picked her and Baby J up, she'd felt safe with him. She glanced into the backseat to make sure that her baby was still asleep before addressing Duke's question.

"I just think it's funny that--"

"Ohhhh, so we on that shit now? I can already tell I'ma need a blunt after this." He chuckled in disbelief, cutting off her sentence and shaking his head.

"What?"

"Bruh, everybody know when a female says that, it's gone be some bullshit, but gone head baby, get it off yo chest now so we can move past it." He looked at her intently for a second and then back at the street ahead. Suddenly, Mercedes felt a little bit embarrassed to even bring up her issue. She wasn't used to a nigga wanting to talk and get shit out the way. With Jermaine, she was constantly asking questions that she already knew the answer to while he ducked and dodged her. Having Duke ready to listen to her and actually come up with a solution had her at a loss. When she still hadn't said anything, he raised an eyebrow and peered over at her again as if prompting her to speak.

"I'm just tryna figure out what we doin'? One minute you in my room kissing and feeling all on me and the next, I hear you fuckin' with a bitch whose hair I do! I mean I know I got a situation, and it probably looks disloyal as fuck for me to be moving on so fast, but I thought maybe...never mind." She stopped herself with a heavy sigh, feeling more and more dumb with each word.

"What bitch?" Duke frowned and she could tell he was trying to figure out which female he fucked with that she might know.

"Raina, she strips down at Blue Flame." It came out much more forcefully than she'd intended, and when he busted out laughing, her lip curled in irritation.

"You tripping girl. I *fuck* Raina from time to time but that's as far as that shit goes. I know her cum guzzlin' ass ain't still flexing like it's anything more than that! Swear these hoes actin' up!"

Mercedes just looked at him blankly, unsure of how to take what he'd just said. On the one hand, she was slightly relieved that it wasn't as serious between them as Raina had made it seem, but on the other hand, she still found herself jealous. It was crazy how territorial she felt over a nigga that she really had no claims to, but she didn't care. As far as she was concerned, Duke was off limits to anyone but her, even if he didn't know it yet.

"So that's what got you walkin' around with yo ass on yo shoulders?" He asked after she still hadn't said anything. Mercedes remained silent choosing not to say anything at the risk of further putting her feelings out there. "So now you ain't got shit to say?"

Again, Mercedes kept her mouth shut as she went over the information he'd just given her in her mind. She was still feeling a way even though he had down played things. It was just like a nigga to make shit seem one way when it was really the complete opposite. He grunted in response to her silence and dropped it, which for some reason further irritated Mercedes.

As soon as they got to the hotel, Duke parked in the closest spot available and she wasted no time getting out and going to the back to grab Baby J out.

"I got him, gone head." Duke said, taking him from her arms the second she turned around. As bad as she wanted to be petty and refuse, the look on his face made her release the hold she had on her baby. Pouting, she followed him into the building and up the elevator. Once she opened her room door, she finally found her voice.

"I can take it from...here." Mercedes voice trailed off as Duke brushed past her and disappeared inside. She wanted to slam the door so bad, but she didn't want to possibly wake Baby J's little bad ass up and have to deal with him once Duke finally left. Shrugging out of her jean jacket, she entered the living room area just as he emerged from the bedroom. "I guess I'll see you later, you can let yourself out." She went to walk around him, but he snatched her right back.

"See, you tryna treat me like yo hoe ass baby daddy, and you can't handle me like you do him. We cut from completely different cloths shorty so believe that when I tell you some shit, that's what it is! I don't even know why we arguing about this shit! That bitch should be the least of your fucking worries when I'm here with you every fuckin' day, putting in work to show you that *I'm* the nigga you need in your life! Why would I even want that ran through bitch when I got you?"

"That all sounds good Duke, but how do I know for sure?"

"Ain't no *buts*, if you tryna be mine then just say that shit! Matter fact, I'm claiming yo ass right now! You *my* woman now, is you finished or is you done?"

Mercedes went to speak and was immediately cut off by Duke crashing his lips into hers. She couldn't lie and say that his whole little speech hadn't had her turned all the way on, and the second that his hands began to roam her body, it was like her floodgates opened and all doubts were gone. Mercedes had never felt that way with Maine, not even in the beginning, which was a whole other reason why she decided to give in to Duke. Totally in tune with one another, they moved throughout the room discarding clothes and exploring each other's bodies until Mercedes found herself straddling his lap as he sat on the couch. She could feel his rock hard dick beneath her and a rush of fear shot through her body at his size.

"Why you so fuckin' wet girl, damn!" Duke grumbled as his applied pressure to her clit and simultaneously kissed her neck. Mercedes fought hard to control the orgasm she felt about to erupt, but as soon as he sucked her left nipple into his mouth and dipped his fingers inside of her, she shuddered.

"Mmmhhh." She moaned and fell against him. Duke gave her a second to recover as he fished a condom out of his pocket and put it on quickly.

"You trust me?" He questioned, nudging her so that she looked down into his handsome face while he rubbed his dick up and down her already drenched slit. The moment was intense and passionate as hell, plus the small amount of pressure he was applying to her already sensitive nub had her ready to combust. Unable to speak from the sheer pleasure of it all, she nodded quickly, ready to feel him. Duke brought his lips to hers again as he entered her slowly, but even that didn't stop the sting of him opening her up. Mercedes felt like she was being split in two and her body instinctively stiffened.

"Duke." She whimpered.

"Don't freeze up on yo dick baby, open up for me." He urged, his voice husky. Mercedes spread her thighs slightly and squeezed her eyes closed as Duke pushed his way fully inside of her, pausing briefly to allow her body to adjust to his size while he distracted her with a deep kiss. Mercedes began to slowly move her hips and the pain quickly gave way to pleasure as Duke reached parts of her body she'd never had touched before. "Ohhh fuck, just like that." He groaned against her lips and slapped her roughly on her ass.

Mercedes tucked her head into his neck, biting him and speeding up as she felt another orgasm rock her core. "Ooooh Duke, I'm comiinng!"

"Catch that nut shorty." Duke encouraged, matching her strokes with his own. He ran his hands up and down her back before settling them in a firm grip on her plump ass. Once he felt her walls contracting around him again, he easily lifted her, turning around so that she was laying halfway off the couch while he knelt before her. Duke had been on the verge of busting just off of how wet and tight Mercedes was, but he'd held himself together. After knowing that she was fulfilled though, he was ready to finally get his.

Mercedes held onto the back of the couch as Duke held her legs in the crooks of his arms, hitting her with long deep strokes that had his dick glistening from her juices. He watched in amazement as her pussy coated the condom, filling the room with sloppy wet noises.

"Ohhhh myyyy gawd Duke! What you doin' tooo meee!" She screeched as her body shook. A cocky grin covered Duke's face; he could already tell that Mercedes was going to be strung out. He hoisted one of her legs onto his shoulder and pulled her closer to him since she'd tried to run away.

"Stop tryna get away, take this dick like a big girl." He growled, nearing his own release. The sound of her moaning as she did what he said and started moving in sync with him brought Duke's nut, shooting out hard enough to come through the condom. He had never nut that hard and long in his life, not even when he'd gotten his first shot of pussy. Duke looked down into Mercedes' face as she lay there still spent from her own orgasm, no doubt while she continued to squeeze the rest of his nut from his body until he eased it out slowly. Maine had fucked up letting a nigga like him anywhere near his bitch. He was ready to kill over Mercedes' ass and he wasn't even ashamed to admit it.

Mercedes felt herself being lifted all the way off of the couch and opened her eyes to meet Duke's, who was giving her a stare so intense that it almost made her nervous.

"On my soul shorty, yo ass bet not *ever* try and dip out on a nigga with pussy that good." He said, causing her to burst into laughter. He cracked a smile of his own, but his eyes said that he wasn't playing.

"Same here, don't be tryna take the dick away from me either." She threatened before giving him a quick kiss.

"Shiiit, where I'm going? You stuck with my ass!" Mercedes didn't mind the sound of that at all. He carried her into the bathroom and they quickly showered.

Once they were both cleaned-- she'd put on a simple pair of cloth shorts with an off the shoulder crop and Duke had slipped back on his boxers and his wife beater--Duke's phone rang. He quickly broke away from the hold he'd had on her and grabbed his work phone out of his jeans pocket.

"What's up?" He answered, running a hand down his waves as she settled on the couch and cut on the TV. She didn't have a class the next day, so she planned on sitting up and hanging out with him for as long as she could because her eyes were already drooping. "What! I'm on my way man!" Mercedes could instantly tell that something was wrong and was proven right when he began to get fully dressed once he'd hung up.

"Is everything okay?" She asked, getting up from the couch to help him as he looked around the room frantically for his other shoe.

"Nah, something happened at one of my houses. I gotta go check that shit out, but I'll be back when I'm finished ayite and don't leave til then." He ordered after she handed him the shoe, which had been by the end table. Whatever was going on clearly had him distracted since he'd missed it sitting right out in the open.

"Okay." Mercedes barely got out before he gave her a quick kiss and was out the door.

26

Anger flamed through Duke's body when he pulled up to his trap to see firefighters, police, and tons of neighbors milling about. They were still fighting the thick flames, so they barely paid him any attention as he got out and walked over, spotting one of his workers standing amongst the crowd.

"What. The. Fuck. Happened?" He gritted between his teeth, barely loud enough for Mills to hear.

"All I know is that Dread hit my line and it sounded like World War three was goin' on in that bitch." Mills told him in a hushed tone. "He was able to tell me that nigga Maine was in there, but before he could tell me shit else, they busted in the room on fam. By the time I got here, it was already up in smoke."

The fact that Maine's name was tied to the shit barely surprised him. The nigga had been cut off and he'd lost his girl and his son, so it was only a matter of time before he snapped, but he hadn't expected him to do something of this magnitude. Duke was sure that he hadn't done it alone though; he just wondered who would have been stupid enough to go on a suicide mission with him. His mind raced as he tried to calculate how much money and product they had lost while he dialed up Major, informing him of what happened. Of course, that nigga was pissed too. That was the second house they'd lost and more money and workers that they had to replace.

"What you want me to do?" Mills asked as soon as he was off the phone. Duke didn't know if Maine planned on hitting up any more of their traps and he didn't want to find out.

"Hit everybody up and let them know that we shutting down the houses until further notice. Tell them to clean everything out and meet us at the warehouse *tonight!*" he emphasized before walking off with his phone to his ear. Duke had almost too many calls to make, in addition to getting his remaining workers on the same page within the next couple hours. He needed to get some money put together for the families of the six niggas who had died that night. Him and Major had some loyal people who had lost their lives behind Maine's bullshit, and he couldn't help feeling guilty about what had happened. He would make sure that he covered their burial expenses and took care of each of their families, but he knew that wouldn't bring them back.

By the time he'd made it back to his car, Duke had handled half of the business and began making calls to niggas at the different houses. Most of them had already heard from Mills, but he had to make sure. Even the workers that weren't working right when the shit popped off needed to be called in so that they all were aware of what was going on. Nobody was allowed to miss the shit and he made that perfectly clear on every call. Maine wanted a war and Duke was ready to give it to him.

Exactly two hours later, him and Major sat in front of a warehouse full of workers. As far as Duke could tell, everyone was in attendance just like he'd wanted and they had all brought what they had from the houses. Major paced back and forth as he barked orders.

"I want that nigga fuckin' head! This the second loss we done took and I don't give a fuck what need to be done so that we don't take another one. Everybody in the city need to be on high alert that if you see that nigga, get his ass! As far as the houses go, give me a week and I'm gone have y'all back up and running! *Do not* disclose the new locations to nobody, not even ya fuckin' baby mamas, not until we catch these bitch ass niggas! Y'all dismissed!" Nobody asked any questions as they all filed out, and Duke turned to him ready to further plan when Yayo came over to where they stood.

"Aye, I don't know if this gone help or not, but them niggas Chris and Petey was MIA today."

"Who the fuck is that?" Major looked Duke's way confused, and he frowned as realization hit him.

"Shit, Chris work at the same house as Mills. He used to work at the one that just got hit, but I moved his ass like a week ago cause he wasn't working fast enough." Duke shrugged. "Who the fuck is Petey though?"

"That's Maine's right hand." Yayo informed them. "If Maine made a move, I can guarantee that nigga helped, but with Chris disappearing, I wouldn't put it past his weird ass to be in cahoots with them niggas." Duke mulled over the information in his head, considering how accurate it might be. Chris had always struck him as a bitch, but he could definitely see him being a *follow the leader* ass nigga. As far as he was concerned, any odd behavior at that point proved guilty to him, and Duke was going to be sure to look into it.

"Good lookin'." He nodded absentmindedly and slapped hands with dude. Major did the same and as soon as Yayo walked off, the two shared a look. It was obvious that they were thinking the same thing.

"I knew we shoulda killed his ass!" Major spat, shaking his head regretfully.

"Man you took the words right out my mouth." Duke agreed with a sigh. "Them niggas dumb as fuck though, and you already know we gone catch them sooner rather than later."

"Still pissed the fuck off, but you right. We just gotta keep our ears to the streets. Eventually, they gone have to come up off that work and when they do, we gone know cause don't shit move in this city without me knowing." Major bumped his fist into Duke's, who was nodding his agreement as he finally paid attention to what the fuck his homey had on.

"Nigga, you out here in some fuckin' pajamas and gym shoes?" He pointed at the plaid pants, tank top, and Jordan's that Major had rolled up in.

"Thugs don't fuckin' wear pajamas muthafucka, these some lounge pants." Major explained with scowl.

"Shit, *thugs* don't wear no fuckin' lounge pants either!"

"Man fuck you! I was in the bed with my girl when you called. I ain't have time to change and shit." He fussed, walking to the door with Duke right behind him. The fact that Major was irritated only made Duke laugh harder as they stopped just outside while he locked up.

"I bet Kiyah's ass probably bought you them shits too huh? I'ma fuck Mercedes up if she ever come to me with anything other than some ball shorts or boxers to sleep in!" Duke continued to crack jokes.

"Yo, you way too worried bout what the fuck I got on nigga, you on some gay shit right now for real! You better take yo goofy ass on." Major cracked, instantly stopping Duke's laughter.

"Yeah ayite nigga, I just slid out the pussy myself."

"So, you giving me down low vibes right now with that funny shit, checkin' a nigga out and shit." Major added insult to injury by giving him the side eye, even though he wanted to fall out laughing from the sour look on his boy's face.

"Ayite man, gone head on with that shit." All joking on Duke's side was gone now and he waved Major off as he got into his car; however, he could still hear Major talking shit.

"Aye don't get salty now! Ain't that what y'all females be sayin'?" Major was damn near bent over in laughter at that point, and Duke peeled out on his ass. He wasn't really mad at his homey, but he wasn't about to play with him talking about him being gay. Once he was on his way back to Mercedes, his thoughts were taken over by how he was going to enjoy killing Maine when he finally got his hands on him, putting him in a better mood than he'd been in since he'd first received the call about his trap. Knowing that he was soon going to get his revenge on that nigga somewhat put him at ease. Or maybe it was the fact that he was on his way back to his girl. Duke didn't know, but either way, he was coming out on top.

❦ 27 ❧

It had been damn near a week since Maine, Chris, and Petey had ran up in the trap, and Maine was still riding a high from that shit. The fact that them niggas still had yet to find him was making Maine feel invincible, and despite Chris's warnings, he'd decided to throw a party. They'd made it out with five keys and damn near a hundred thousand dollars and were still alive to tell it. That was more than enough of a reason to celebrate and that's exactly what Maine planned on doing. They'd invited some strippers and had their hotel room full of weed smoke and bottles everywhere.

"Nigga, this shit lit!" Petey exclaimed excitedly while two bitches danced in his lap, damn near fucking each other.

"Hell yeah! Ain't this what I told you it was gone be like?" Maine bragged, puffing on the fat ass blunt he had between his lips. He felt like *the man* and couldn't nobody tell him different. Being able to see the looks on Major and Duke's faces when they saw their precious trap burning to the ground and knowing that they'd lost money was almost enough to give him a hard on. He took a swig from the bottle of D'usse that he was holding and played *"Ran off on the Plug twice"* for like the hundredth time that night, instantly getting lit as soon as the beat dropped. Not even Chris sitting in the corner pouting could bring down his mood.

"Trap money made six figures, if you thuggin' out, you better keep a rocket with ya!" Maine stood in the middle of the floor rapping the lyrics and throwing money into the air that had the strippers in the room scrambling. Him and Petey shared a laugh while Chris huffed and shook his head.

"Y'all niggas up in here actin' like shit all good and blowing money that we just got on some stripper hoes! Do you really think this shit is smart considering--"

"Aye man, shut the fuck up! Take yo ass home with that scary shit!" Maine barked, getting in his face, and just like the punk Maine knew he was, Chris immediately backed down and snatched up his shit, leaving the room.

"Man, don't trip about his scary ass... we good and we got Bullet behind us if anybody got a problem." Petey voiced, talking about the head of the Get Low boys. Maine nodded, despite feeling a tiny bit worried due to Chris's words. As much as he wanted to pretend, he couldn't deny knowing that if Duke and Major found out it was him that had robbed them, he was as good as dead, probably even with the support of Bullet. Maine took a long sip from his bottle and looked around the room with a frown.

"Aye, where them other bitches go?" He asked the remaining two strippers that were in the room dancing around. They were alright, but as far as strippers went, the two that were missing were the finest bitches he'd ever seen but not as bad as his baby mama. . As soon as Maine saw them enter the room, he'd laid claim to them and had full intentions on fucking them both before the night was out.

"They in the bathroom, but why you care when you got all this out here?" The stripper known as Butterscotch said, coming over to him and placing his hand on her ass. Maine let it linger there for a second or two but then pulled away.

"I care cause unlike what niggas tell you, pussy *do* got a face, and I ain't tryna fuck neither one of you dog faced broads!" He spat, disrespectfully ignoring their shocked gasps and going straight over to the bathroom door. Maine listened from the outside, hoping to hear some kind of movement because they'd been feeding them bitches all types of molly, liquor, and coke, and the last thing he needed was a bitch overdosed in his room.

"Bitch, I swear to God I'm gone fuck Duke and that bitch Mercedes up! I just brought that nigga's name up to her and told her we was fuckin' around, now all of a sudden she postin' him on her Instagram!"

"How you even know her?! She look like she think she too good to hang with bitches like us." The other girl smacked her lips. Maine leaned in a little closer, hoping to hear more. As much as the thought of Duke fucking his most prized possession irritated him, he knew that if he continued to listen without reacting, he may have a chance at getting her back.

"She does my fucking hair. The bitch do a good job too... it's too bad I'm gone break her fucking fingers for touching my nigga!" The first girl threatened, causing the other one to laugh. Little did the bitch know, she wasn't going to lay a hand on Mercedes if Maine could help it. He chose that moment to push the door open, glad to find that it wasn't locked. They both froze up the second they saw that it was him and not one of the other strippers, but he gave them an easy grin to let them know it was cool.

"Did I hear you say Mercedes?" He looked between the two girls, unsure of who had brought up his baby mama's name until he saw the lighter of the them sneer at his question. "Save all that shorty, Mercedes' my baby mama and the way I see it, we can help each other out. I want her and if you help me get her, I'll make sure she stay away from yo dude." She peered at him skeptically before looking at her friend, who merely shrugged and threw her hands up. After thinking it over, the sly smile on her face showed that she was willing to go along with whatever he had in mind. Maine saw all thirty two of her teeth as she held her hand out to him.

"Raina." She introduced herself happily. "And this is Stormi." She pointed back towards her friend.

"Maine." He stuck his hand inside of hers, grinning also because shorty didn't even know that he was going to kill her stupid ass as soon as she got him what he wanted.

"Now what did you have in mind?"

28

Graduation was over and it was time for the next phase in Kiyah's life. She was nervous but excited nonetheless. The only thing that she had an issue in her life at that moment was that her parents weren't too fond of Major and she was head over heels for his ass. Things had been going so great for them. Kiyah had been at the point where she said fuck love, but his smooth ass swooped in right on time and swept her off of her feet. He was handsome, smart, had a great personality, had a little thug in him, which made her feel safe, and the sex was bomb as fuck. Kiyah didn't plan on letting him go because that combination only existed in urban fiction books.

"I can't believe you won't be in the city no more," Mercedes pouted.

"I knoowww, but you know you can visit anytime you want, and Major lives here so you know I'll be back and forth," Kiyah winked.

"Major came in and swept yo ass off yo feet fast as hell," Mercedes noted.

"Bout the same as Duke did yo ass," Kiyah laughed.

"I guess you right... that man done made me forget all about Maine.

I can't even begin to describe the sex girrlll... Oh my gawwddd!!" Mercedes beamed.

"Oh, I see that glow. I'm just happy that you found someone who respects you and makes you happy," Kiyah asserted and then she noticed the look on Mercedes' face.

"What's wrong?" Kiyah quizzed.

"I know you gon' say I'm overthinking and shit, but I can't help but to feel like this shit is too good to be true... or something bad gon' happen," Mercedes divulged.

Kiyah paused before replying. She wanted to think things through before saying anything. Normally, she was the one who was trying to shoot off the positive vibes, but deep down, she honestly felt like something was about to happen too. She had yet to reveal the information she found out about Chris to anyone. The shit had her spooked, but the good thing about it in her eyes, she was moving and she didn't have any more classes with him. She really couldn't believe he had her damn panties hanging on the door and had pictures of them that had never been taken. Shit was crazy as fuck.

"Duke, ain't gon' let shit happen to you girl. Fuck Maine bitch ass," Kiyah finally expressed.

"Yeah you right... fuck him," she could tell Mercedes was trying to convince herself.

Before I Let Go by Beyoncé sounded and it was a great distraction for the friends. They sang and danced around while packing up clothes and waiting on the movers. By the time the song was over, they both had worked up a sweat. As soon as the song ended, Kiyah's phone rang and she knew it was her mom by the ringtone.

"Hey ma!" she answered.

"Hey sweetie. How are you?"

"I'm good. Me and Mercedes just chillin' and packing up my stuff."

"You never said what day you were actually moving. When is it so we can come down and help?"

"Wellll, I actually wanted to surprise you guys and be settled next time y'all come. I'm moving today," Kiyah blurted.

"TODAY? Wow Kiyah... this new man has changed you. I bet he

knows you're moving. He's probably helping while we're left stuck looking like outsiders," Karen scolded.

"Wow mom... just wow! I knew dad wasn't feeling Major, but I thought you at least understood. I gotta go. I'll talk to you later," Kiyah hung up before her mom could make her feel any worse.

Kiyah couldn't lie, her parents not liking Major had her in her feelings. She can't lie and say that she didn't expect it a little, but it still hurt nonetheless. The fact that she was grown and they raised her but didn't trust her judgment spoke volumes. A tear threatened to escape her left eye, but Kiyah blinked it back up. She refused to take it there at that moment. Not telling her parents didn't have a thing to do with Major, and she wasn't about to be guilt tripped into believing it did.

"Now you know your parents... don't even sweat that Kiy. Mama Karen will apologize. It might take longer for your dad, but you know that already too," Mercedes rubbed her back.

"You're right. It's just frustrating though," Kiyah sighed.

"I know it is, but it's gonna all work out sis. Be positive and stop stressing... just like you be telling me."

"Look at you...tryna be me and shit. Let's finish up so we can grab something to eat before riding out to Duluth," Kiyah beseeched.

The girls got back into their groove of singing and dancing and they had everything packed and labeled within the hour. As soon as they finished, a call came through on Kiyah's phone. She answered and it was the movers. After confirming that everything was a go, Kiyah ended the call and her and Mercedes headed out.

"I kinda want some seafood. You cool wit that?" Kiyah waited to see if Mercedes was good with her food choice.

"Yeah that's fine."

Thirty minutes later, Kiyah turned into Spondovitis. There was an empty space right near the front, so she swooped into it and they were inside in no time. The restaurant was always packed, but since it was a weekday, the wait time wasn't too long. Once they were seated, their waitress approached them a few minutes later and Kiyah and Mercedes ordered their drinks, appetizers, and entrees all at one time. Kiyah decided on Cajun shrimp as an appetizer while Mercedes ordered fried calamari. They ordered the deluxe seafood platter to share as their entrée, even though they were going to share everything anyway.

"This is Ms. Jones calling, I hope ain't nothing wrong," Mercedes panicked as she answered her phone.

When Kiyah saw her smiling, she knew that everything was all good and she was elated. She took that opportunity to excuse herself to go to the bathroom. After relieving her bladder and washing her hands, Kiyah exited the bathroom and bumped into the asshole that broke her heart. She turned her nose up at him and walked around him, but he grabbed her arm. The look she gave him let him know to remove his hands with the quickness and he did just that.

"You look good Kiyah," he complimented.

"Thanks," she replied, making the quick decision not to consume any negative energy because if him. If it wasn't for him, she wouldn't have Major so she was happy.

"I see I still make you smile," he cockily stated.

"Yeah, if you wouldn't have fucked up, I wouldn't have met a *real* man. So thank you... now goodbye," Kiyah rolled her eyes and walked away, ignoring her name being called.

A few hours later, Kiyah turned into the driveway of her new home. The house was nice and she was already in love with it, but the one next door was breathtakingly beautiful.

"Damn friend, I wonder who stay there. That's gotta be a celebrity's house or some shit. This neighborhood is nice as fuck. I'ma be like you when I grow up." Mercedes teased.

"Girl stop. That shit is bad though, and we only see the outside," Kiyah said as she parked.

"Bad is an understatement. If we both wasn't boo'd up already, I'd be saying we need to see who the fuck that is," Mercedes laughed.

"I know I keep saying this and I'm probably sounding like a broken record, but it's so good to see you happy friend. Duke done brought out the person I knew was deep within all these years," Kiyah smiled at her friend.

Before Mercedes could answer, Kiyah's phone rang and it made her smile since it was Major calling.

"Heeyyy you," she gushed.

"Hey babe. Everything good?" he asked.

"Yup. Me and Mercedes just made it to my new place. We just bout to get out and go inside. I'll drop my location to you. Where you at?"

"I had to come and grab some shit out my safe. Shoot me that location so I can see how far it is," Major replied.

"Okay hold on."

Kiyah took the phone from her ear and dropped her location to Major. Before letting him know she sent it, something caught her eye and she nudged Mercedes and pointed.

"You on Lockley Pass in Duluth?" Kiyah asked him.

"Damn, you stalking a nigga?" he laughed but she could tell that he was shook a lil bit.

"Nah, but you just pulled up right next door," Kiyah noted and got out the car.

Major stopped his truck and rolled the window down.

"No this nigga don't live next door to yo ass," Mercedes laughed, but Kiyah had some questions.

29

As she looked in the mirror and fixed the stray hairs in her silk press, Mercedes felt like she was on cloud nine. Not only had she managed to get out of her crazy ass situation, but she had found a good ass man and her business was booming. She had a healthy glow to her cheeks and she knew it was due to Duke. Mercedes did a slight twerk in the mirror and took a picture for her Instagram before stepping out of the bathroom. Duke and Baby J were in the bed knocked out since it was her baby's nap time, but she took the risk of snapping a picture of them anyway.

"Stop taking pictures and bring yo ass here so I can get a kiss before you leave." Duke mumbled without opening his eyes. It was crazy how well he knew her in such a short period of time. His ass wasn't even all the way awake and yet, he knew she was in the room with her phone poised. Giggling, she made her way over to the side of the bed that he was on and bent to press her lips against his.

"Ahhh!" She squealed as he pulled her on top of him, holding her firmly so that she couldn't get up.

"You bet not wake this lil nigga up! I'm tryna at least get a hour of sleep before I get to moving this shit!" Duke whispered into her ear as his hands ran the length of her body, stopping on her ass.

"I told you I ain't staying over there that close to Maine, so leave my shit right where it's at." She warned, kissing him between each word. Ever since the night that he'd claimed her body, Duke had been pressuring Mercedes to move in with him and Dreka. She had tried explaining to him that he lived way too close to her ex for her to move around unnoticed, and she also felt like it was too soon to live together when she'd just found her freedom. Immediately, his eyes popped open at her refusal and he pinned her with an irritated expression.

"You don't think I can protect you from that nigga? That's what you tryna say?"

Mercedes smoothed out the crease that had appeared on his forehead with her finger and rolled her eyes. She hated when he doubted her faith in him, especially where Maine was concerned.

"I *know* you can protect me, protect us, but I just don't think it's a good idea right now. Look, I gotta go or I'm gone be late to do this girl hair, but when I get back, we can talk about it some more." Mercedes promised, staring into his eyes in awe. Duke was so fucking handsome, she almost always found it hard to believe that he had decided to be with her; a girl who came with tons of baggage and wasn't nearly on the same playing field financially, but she was getting there. He released a deep sigh and gave her a firm squeeze before kissing her deeply and letting her go.

"Bet." He eyed her once she stood to her feet and smoothed out the yellow bodysuit she wore and her high waisted fashion nova jeans. "Damn girl, you look good as fuck. I almost don't even wanna let yo ass leave." His voice lowered as he took her in from head to toe, tucking his lip between his teeth. Mercedes blushed and clenched her thighs together, knowing that if she fed into his flirting she would never get out of there. That was another thing that was refreshing about Duke. He wasn't insecure about her going out looking good. Being cared for by him the way she was made it so easy to turn other niggas down. That was something that Maine had never understood; he always felt like she should only look good for him inside their home. If she dared step outside looking like she gave a fuck about herself, then he was instantly jealous. Mercedes didn't miss those dark days and more and more, she was living the life that she felt God had intended for her.

"When I get back, you can keep me here all day, but I don't wanna fuck up with a new client." A girl named Nessa had messaged her earlier that week for a hair do. She said that Raina had referred her, and despite Mercedes still feeling a way about the shit Raina said concerning Duke, she didn't plan on letting it fuck with her money.

"You sure you cool goin' by yourself? I can take you if you want."

"Nope, you ain't even slick! Yo ass just scared to let me drive, but I'll be straight bae and I'll see you in a couple hours. Two tops." She hurried to blow him a kiss and was out the door before he could object. She excitedly hopped into the driver's seat of his G-wagon and cut on some Cardi B as she pulled out of the parking lot. It felt so good to be out driving with no time limit on when she needed to be back.

It didn't even take her a half hour before she was pulling up at the address the girl had sent to her. She squinted at the building wondering if she might have gotten it wrong, but when she texted Nessa, she assured her that it was right and even came out onto the front porch to wave her over. Mercedes shrugged off the weird vibe she was getting and climbed out with her cosmetology bag in tow.

"Hey girl! I'm glad you could fit me in. I swear I been needing my shit touched up so bad." She gushed the second Mercedes came up the stairs.

"No problem Nessa. For real, you're really helping me out."

"Well, I always try and support, but you can call me Stormi, Nessa is just my Instagram name." She slipped her hand into Mercedes and then led her inside. Almost instantly, Mercedes felt that something wasn't right. Her apartment was virtually empty aside from a torn up couch, and as bad as she wanted to not judge her, it really looked abandoned inside.

"You know what? I uh... I forgot my flat irons in the car. I'm just gone go grab them quick." Mercedes said, starting for the door, but Stormi stepped in front of it and set the locks. She stared at her unapologetically with her arms folded and Mercedes quickly dropped her bag, ready to fight the bitch if she had to when the last voice she was expecting to hear came from behind her, breaking the silence.

"Why you tryna leave so soon, didn't you miss yo man?" Cringing, Mercedes turned around, already knowing what she would see when she did. Her eyes landed on Maine and everything went black.

❧ 30 ❧

It had been almost a week since Kiyah moved into her new place. Major couldn't believe the damn chances that she was really setup right next door to him. If it had not been for her living in the city, he would have been at his home out in Duluth more, but the need and want to be close to her outweighed all that shit. She tried to cop a lil attitude like he lied to her or some shit about where he lived, but after he dicked her down, she came back to her senses. Maine's ass was still hiding under a rock, but Major knew that it was only a matter of time before he slipped up so they could put him six feet under. If he could turn back the hands of time, he would let Duke kill that nigga and not think twice about it. But, life don't work like that. Major's phone rang while he was driving and he let the Bluetooth pick up.

"What up?" he answered, not bothering to pick up the phone and look to see who was calling.

"Hey big head!" Yanna squealed.

"What up sis? How you feeling?"

"I'm fiiiine... can you pleeaasseee tell mommy and daddy I'm fine too so they can stop treating me like a baby?" he could hear the irritation in her voice and he laughed.

"It ain't funny. They acting like they don't even want me to drive no more... like the shit was my fault," Yanna continued.

"They just tryna keep you safe. They'll ease up soon sis. Just relax."

"Yeah yeah yeah... so when can I come visit? I ain't been there in forever because you always popping up here. Plus, I wanna see Kiyah. She cool as hell."

It was true, Major always popped up at home because he didn't want anyone laying eyes on his people and targeting them. His dad was the exception to the rule because his ass popped up whenever the hell he wanted to. Thinking about the situation with Maine had Major knowing that he couldn't be distracted.

"I ain't gon' be in yo way... plus I can kick it wit Kiyah. I already booked a flight. I need a break from here," Yanna interrupted his thoughts.

"Yanna, how the hell you gon' book a flight before asking?"

"Because you my brother and I miss you... I gotta take this call. I'll be there tomorrow bye," she hung up before Major could say anything else.

He knew that it was no use in calling Yanna back because her ass wasn't gonna answer. Since Kiyah was out in Duluth and not in the city, it might be okay for her visit. Major kept thinking about the situation and concluded that Yanna and Kiyah would be fine. They could do some girly shit with Mercedes while him and Duke handled business. He turned into Kiyah's driveway and parked behind her car. They had a Friday night date night that she pretty much forced him into. He killed his engine and got out. She opened the door dressed in a black panty and bra lace set.

"Let me throw on my clothes," she turned to leave, but Major snatched her ass up.

"Hell naw... you got my dick hard as fuck now. How you gon' open the door dressed like that?" he fondled with her breasts and then began kissing on them.

Before long, Major's face was buried deep between Kiyah's legs. He sucked up her pussy juices and made her cum back to back in his mouth. She tasted so fuckin' sweet that he could eat her all day and night. His throbbing hard dick had other plans at that moment, so

Major eased up and slid inside his pussy. Kiyah's moans got louder and louder and the shit made him harder. She had learned to take the dick better, but he still got the best of her nine times out of ten.

"Oh shiiitttt!" Kiyah screamed as Major went deep.

She pushed at his stomach, but he ignored her pleas and kept fucking her.

"You... knew... what... you... was... doing," he said between strokes.

"Whhaaatttt?" Kiyah squealed like she didn't know what he was talking about.

She clenched her pelvic muscles and found the strength to throw it back one good time at Major. That sent him over the edge. He exploded inside of her and collapsed on top.

"Damn boy... you would think you wasn't getting no pussy," Kiyah laughed.

"I'm addicted to that good thang," he rolled over, smacking her on her thigh.

"Come on... let's go wash up so we can go," Kiyah pulled him up.

"Where we goin' anyway? You never said."

"I know you too much of a thug to do the movies, so I figured we could go to Top Golf."

"I'm too much of a thug for that shit too," he mumbled.

"Well yo thuggish ass finna go today," she fired back.

Thirty minutes later, they were dressed in black and white Adidas track suits and were out the door. Kiyah told him that she had picked the outfits up from her old job a couple days ago, and he told her that she had him looking like a high school kid dressing alike and shit; but she only snapped pics and ignored his ass. They hopped in the car and headed back towards the city. Forty minutes into the drive, Major's phone rang and he allowed it to be answered on Bluetooth like he normally did while driving.

"What up?"

"Hey."

Major caught Nisha's voice instantly.

"What up Nish? You done dropped that load yet?"

"Yeah. I had MJ a few days ago," Kinisha confessed.

"Well congrats... shit been crazy, but I'll get my girl to send you some gifts for lil man, and we'll get by there to see him when you ready for visitors."

"Good because I need you to sign the birth certificate so I can give our son your last name."

"What the fuck? Nisha... you high or some shit?" Major fumed.

He could feel Kiyah staring a hole in the side of his head and saw her leg shaking out of the corner of his eye.

"Nah, I ain't high and I lied... he *is* your son. For sure."

"What the fuck kinda games..."

RATATATAT RATATATAT RATATATAT

Gunfire rang out, causing Major to lose control of the truck. Swerving into oncoming traffic, the last thing Major heard before flipping over and succumbing to darkness were terrifying distress screams from Kiyah.

TO BE CONTINUED...

ACKNOWLEDGMENTS

This one is for our wonderful supporters! We appreciate each and every single one of you. Much love, always!! :)

Made in the USA
Monee, IL
26 February 2020